REALM WALKER

Hidden Passages

Elle Klass

Hidden Passages

Copyright©2023 by Elle Klass
Published by Books by Elle, Inc.
ISBN: 978-1-951017-40-8
All rights reserved
Editor Dawn Lewis
Cover art Getcovers.com

Author's Disclaimer

This book is entirely fictional. Any characters or events are purely figments of the author's imagination. City and business names are fictional as well. No part of this publication may be reproduced, transmitted or redistributed either in its entirety or in part without the author's express written consent.

Realm Walker

Books in the Realm Walker Series
In the Shadows
The Land of Lost Souls
Hidden Passages
The Ring of Betrayal

Other Realm Walker Companion Books
The Origin: Marya's Journal
Soul Fire

Realm Walker World Books – coming soon!
Love at Frost Bite
Accidental Ghost: Soul Catcher Vol.1

Other Young Adults Series
The Bloodseeker
Zombie Girl
Hidden Journals
Baby Girl

REALM WALKER

1

Latisha – Northeastern Regional Warlock Wizard

Latisha shuddered with a pinched face as she closed the periwinkle blue curtains. The dark nymphs, with their razor-sharp teeth and springs of unkempt hair that stood out at all angles, were the most disgusting creatures she'd ever seen. She understood why they stayed hidden and were the creatures of most human childhood nightmares.

They weren't more than two inches in height, but carried the stench of rotting flesh. Stuffing a rag to her nose, she reached under the sink and sprayed her quarters with air freshener.

Dropping the rag from her nose, she stuffed it into the laundry chute by the long, silver dresser. Latisha couldn't sit still as she paced from one end of her private quarters to the other. A velvet chaise, also the color of periwinkle, sat beneath a large window covered by the curtains she'd pulled shut. The recessed lights decreased in brightness as she turned the knob to help her focus by limiting distractions.

All shades of blue pillows were laid against the headboard of the silver bed frame. The bed made to perfection, with zero wrinkles. The other end of the room housed her massive closet. Through the closet, a door was built into a fake wall that led to her office and their formal meeting room.

She clenched her fists then released as she let out a deep breath. She could almost smell Marsidia. The Stones of Hovrath were last known to be in the fae lands, and they were finally taking them back. Warlocks had waited so long and now she could taste it. The light at the end of the tunnel within reach, but a lot could go wrong and she didn't completely trust her sources.

Dark nymphs weren't reliable, but they were tiny enough to slip through the veil, undetected and undeterred. There were small gaps and cracks. The map they drew, and their intel, matched the stories of her ancestors. Their intel filled with the secrets of the other species. It was their weaknesses Latisha found most helpful, especially the larger and more vicious species.

She had warlocks with the sun rune waiting for her command if there was any vampire trouble. They wouldn't create enough to fry every vampire, but would be able to send a powerful message and, if the warlocks banded together, they could shine as bright as the sun for a limited amount of time.

She didn't fool herself; the large and vicious species were a threat, but so were the others. All her forces carried silver swords should wolves become a problem and, according to the nymphs, vampire blood killed dragons.

Even the lesser species she took care of. Iron bullets would take out a fae and dreadwood grenades would subdue the elves. Dreadwood didn't grow on Earth, but the nymphs were helpful enough to bring some back, concentrated; and concentrated could do some damage.

The weapons that made her laugh were the water machine guns and rounds made of concentrated seawater to melt the trolls' skin off their short, squat little bodies. It wasn't her plan to use any weapons, but she never went in unprepared.

The nymphs asked only for passage to Marsidia. It was a small gift for all their intel.

She hoped she didn't regret the decision later, as dark nymphs were known to stir trouble.

The wild card, she figured, were the wolves. They were a hotheaded group, making them untrustworthy and likely not to follow orders. To get them onboard, she had to give them something. Winston wanted land and a pact that neither warlocks nor vampires could cross onto their lands. There'd be consequences if they did. That demand didn't make her skin crawl, it was the other demand – give them the ability to shift at will without pain.

Only the eldest werewolves had the ability to shift on command without excruciating pain. Younger werewolves lacked that control; the phases of the moon controlling their shift. Under full and new moons, they shifted completely, and at other times of the month, a partial shift. All shifts caused discomfort at the least, and pain at the worst.

Hiram readily agreed, for if it wasn't for the warlocks the vampires would still be in the dark ages, only able to come out at night. The agreement the warlocks made with the vampires had proved fruitful over the years and their relationship grew, but she wasn't naïve enough to believe Hiram wouldn't go behind her back for the health of the vampire clans.

REALM WALKER

A team of adult warlocks with the invisibility rune waited on her command. Latisha's dark eyes glanced to the clock, and she let out a deep, sluggish breath. Her double chin bounced like jelly with the movement. Why did the clock move so slowly when waiting? The plan was to surround the fae on each side and take back what was stolen from the warlocks centuries ago. She wanted them to pay.

The approach was three-pronged, and all teams would enter at the same moment. Warlocks with the invisibility rune would enter the land of the elves, vampires the land of the fae, and wolves the land of trolls. In her long life, she'd only dreamt of this moment.

It was that blood boiling vengeance that led her to trust Hiram to extract information from the fae. The vampires' ability to manipulate the mind was superior to the warlocks'. It was as if it was part of the vampire by design.

The vampires weren't clouded by vengeance or anger. If she'd have sent in warlocks with the telepath rune, their judgements may have been blinded with anger, making them less effective in prying information and more likely to kill. She didn't necessarily want all the fae dead, at least not until they suffered. It was the Stones of Hovrath and safe passage to Marsidia for all warlocks who chose to return to their ancestral home that she yearned for so much she could taste the sweetness in the back of her throat.

She had no ill will toward the elves or trolls. The warlocks and wolves were sent merely to secure the border, so none escaped.

With a circular wave of her hand, she watched as her warlocks struck the weak veil of the realm with lightning. She doubted a single elf would notice, as the lightning was concentrated to one area, then spread high above their clouds.

Winston – Northeastern Pack Leader

Winston wasn't sold on the plan or the pact between the wolves, warlocks, and vampires. He'd take the land if Latisha came through, but didn't trust her. Control over shifting he'd thrown in for good measure, and she'd agreed. He laughed inwardly, as she understood so little about his kind. Wolves weren't weak; it was the pain every change of the moon's cycle that gave them strength, honor, and courage.

His true solace was the confirmation that one of his wolves hadn't bitten the young vampire, as he'd insisted from the beginning. Rage burned inside him, his wolf begging to come out. Whoever these other creatures were, they had no business in his territory and causing his pack strife. How dare a wolf in another realm bite a vampire?! He tempered his rage. It would do him no good, not yet, and when all was done his wolves would be released from the curse of the moon. They'd have the freedom and land to shift and hunt at will.

As the alpha, he couldn't deny the existence of the other realms and the threat they posed. How dare they travel to and from his realm? It was high time these other realms understood exactly who they were dealing with. He wanted a piece of them. To sink his own teeth into one and watch as the poison from his bite blackened their veins and swelled their face and extremities.

His wolves, men and women, heads held high, shoulders squared, looked upon him. Tonight, the other realms would know his kind – Earth kind - existed. Light energy hissed and cracked from the palms of warlocks, creating a portal. A warlock stretched the portal so it was large enough an army of wolves could slip in under the cover of night and position themselves to secure the border.

With pride, he watched as his wolves filed into the other realm.

The fae weren't his concern. The vampires were and, now that they were inside these mystery realms, he'd find a way to get to the vampires. The map of these realms, although incomplete, showed the vampire realm was close. He sent a small team of his best soldiers to find it.

He flashed his emerald eyes at Ryoni and slicked a hand through his dirty blonde hair. Ryoni gave a short nod as she and four others hung back. The warlock stayed by Winston's side. He was needed to open a portal back to Earth, but Winston knew he was also a spy for Latisha, the warlocks' regional wizard.

Each member of the pack had a job, and all were loyal to Winston. If the warlock became a problem, they'd take care of it.

Hiram – Northeastern Vampire Clan Leader

The allegiance between the warlocks and vampires was fruitful. It was warlock spells that allowed vampires to walk in the daylight and live freely among the humans. The vampires in the other realm were weak to sunlight, according to the young warlock. It was also reported the land was flowing in blood – human blood.

Hiram swept a chunk of dark hair from his forehead as he leaned over the partial map of the fae realm. His vampires could walk in the sun, allowing them an advantage over other vampires. They would overtake a land of islands and lavender oceans. It was imperative to stay in line with the warlocks, as he wanted a truce with the vampire realm.

It was give and take. He gave Latisha what she wanted with the fae, and he could work a deal with the other vampire leader. He'd promise that leader the ability to walk in the sun, and his vampires would be able to come and go freely.

"We should portal directly to the palace, to the dungeon," Freya said as she studied the same incomplete map of the fae realm. She smoothed her hands over the body-hugging jogging pants covering her legs.

The map of the realm may be incomplete, but they had a solid map of the palace, including how the beings in that realm were working on a potion to seal the veils between Lols and the other realms. Lols – an odd name for Earth.

It was that information bringing them to where they were now. The veils were the invisible barriers between the realms. The plan had been to study the realms long enough to learn about the creatures, magic, customs, and build complete maps, but they no longer had that luxury. This had to be done before they were shut out forever.

Hiram lifted his eyes from the map. "Make sure you cover all the exits." He met Freya's eyes. She was a warrior, one of the best. He shifted his gaze to Grayson. His salt and pepper hair tied back neatly, his long ponytail falling over his shoulder. "When you get the all clear from Freya's team, you will portal into the King and Queen's chamber and secure them."

Grayson nodded. He had the uncanny ability to interrogate with his mind. The plan wasn't to harm the King and Queen, at least not yet. It was to pry information from them. Grayson wouldn't be alone; as he hijacked their minds, cat shifters would infiltrate the rest of the palace, meeting Freya's team halfway until it was secure.

2

Terra

Clyde scampered up the tree and flew off, tackling the chimu. They rolled to a stop at the porch steps, where Terra sat on a porch swing. Chimu were nearly the same size as a ferret, but had a face more like a house cat.

Terra glanced away from Clyde for a second to take the hot chocolate Rosette handed her. Rosette made good on her promise to bring Terra to Meridan forest in Aradia. It had real seasons and, in the middle of fall, the breeze was chilly and felt good against Terra's skin. The air mingled with the scents from many different plants. It was sweet and fresh.

Rosette even made sure to bring commoner food for Terra to eat, instead of forcing vegetarian elf delicacies on her. Tiny white marshmallows floated on the top of the hot chocolate, surrounded by a frothy cream. She lifted the mug to her lips. Steam rose into her nostrils, causing her to glance again at the drink. It bubbled wildly, as if boiling on a stove.

Weird. A minute ago, it hadn't been boiling. Studying the drink, she couldn't figure it out. Rosette was drinking tea; not boiling tea, but hot tea. She set the cup on the table between her and Rosette to give it time to cool as she focused again on Clyde.

"He's made a friend," Rosette noted out loud.

"He's made a family of friends," Terra corrected, as the ferret and three chimu rolled together on the bluish-colored grass. Some trees in Aradia dropped their leaves, while others were evergreen, but not like the spiky evergreens in Lols. These had soft leaves, actual leaves. The leaves changing color were brilliant in crimson red, royal blue, and deep purple. Mixed with the leaves that didn't change, the woods were filled with color.

Bushes bloomed around the trees in similar colors and, at night, the sarcantha flowers made a showy, glowing display of blue. She remembered them from the elf party she crashed a few weeks ago. In Provence, everything would look as it did when they left yesterday. By Monday, when they returned, there'd be no change. No colorful leaves, glowing flowers, fresh air. She sighed.

It was still early as the sun dropped behind the trees. "Is this where you and my mom played?" Terra asked, remembering the memories Rosette shared from her comicay – a gel-like communication device they wore above their wrist.

"It is. Those trees went on endlessly. We'd run through them." Her face suddenly lit up like a little girl. "If we go now, I can show you something more beautiful." Rosette stood, excitement in her voice.

Terra glanced at her hot chocolate that was no longer boiling. She'd drink it cold when they returned. Rosette took her through the woods. Under the trees, green and yellow mushrooms gave off light similar to the sarcantha, but not as bright.

The trail through the woods went up a small rolling hill overlooking a brook. The sky colors matched the leaves and blended over the water in a breathtaking display. Various colors of leaves and flower petals floated on the surface of the water, moving with the current. Beyond the beauty in front of her, something else caught her eye. A stretch of thick trees, their leaves green and flopping over one another. "What's over there?" she asked, pointing.

"You can see that?" Rosette asked, raising a brow.

Sometimes she forgot, as a hybrid elf that was also dragon and some other things, she had acute vision. "Predator genes." The predator subspecies were the dragons, vampires, and lycans.

Rosette's face pinched. "It's the darklands. No one has gone there for centuries, but it's said the first elves to settle in Aradia lived there." There was something in her voice that said she was holding back.

What was she holding back? A high school rendezvous with a bad boy elf? Rosette was so uptight, Terra had a difficult time seeing her as a teen even though she'd seen pictures from her comicay. "Were you ever tempted?"

"Not me," Rosette spat out as if guilty.

Terra didn't linger. If it was a place no one went to, it was the kind of place she wanted to visit. It also gave her other ideas. According to Rosette, her family found her mom in Meridan forest as a baby. She was a hybrid, part elf and part... Terra wasn't sure. The residents of the realms didn't, and don't, like hybrids. Rosette's family took in Terra's mom, raised her as their own. "Could my mom have been from there?"

Rosette thought for a moment, as if figuring out how to respond. "I don't think so." She patted the bottom of her large, bat-wing hair. It cast a shadow on the grass behind her.

Terra focused her vision on the darklands. Not her normal vision, but the one that allowed her to see things others couldn't. The maps she saw were becoming more detailed and dimensional. In the beginning, she saw gridded maps. Today she saw massive tree trunks, thick as a sequoia. Huge thorns and sticky brambles surrounded the woods as if to keep elves out.

No matter how much effort she put in, she wasn't able to see inside the forest. Beyond the forest was Navarin – realm of the fae. The golden sky over the sea was barely visible. Terra wasn't too anxious to ever return. The lavender-colored seas and seafoam green sand were pretty at first, but after several minutes they were nauseating and the yippy doglike energy from the realm, coupled with the colors, was enough to turn her stomach. Aradia had soft energy, like a cat's purr.

Clyde had ridden her shoulder there, worn out from playing with the chimu. He rested his head beneath her chin as the last of the sun lowered beneath the horizon. Solaflies sparkled from the trees, but stayed hidden in the brush. A few weeks ago, they were everywhere. Maybe they didn't like the cold. Terra wrapped her arms around her chest.

Hidden Passages

Spending the weekend with Rosette hadn't been so bad. In Provence, the tribunal decided to allow the commoners, or humans, Terra brought from the Land of Lost Souls, or Lols for short, to stay and attend Provence Academy so they could learn about the realms and how to be tribunal diplomats. Lols was the only realm not represented and Terra thought to change that.

Terra herself was from Lols. She hadn't learned of the realms, or any of the subspecies, until her father passed. Not a day went by she didn't think of him. He was a fire dragon and her mom a hybrid who passed as an elf. According to Rosette, they escaped to Lols when Terra's mom got pregnant with her.

Every time thoughts of her mom entered her head, she thought of the pink carnation tattoo on her ankle and faux pains stabbed at her. It was there to represent the love from the mom she never knew. Nostalgic thoughts were interrupted when she suddenly felt dizzy and stumbled as if drunk, followed by a pain that shot over her torso.

The sky suddenly turned dark, and streaks of blue and violet lightning spread over it, crackling from one end to the next. Instinctively, she opened her predator vision and watched in horror and agony as the veils in the lower realms of Aradia, Verboten, and Navarin appeared to split wide open.

She dropped in pain. Clyde ran up to her knees and lifted his front paws as he sniffed at her face.

"Terra," Rosette's voice broke through the fog in her brain. "What's happening? Are you OK?" Honest concern flowing in her words.

"I'm…" No, she wasn't OK, and didn't understand what was happening. Is this what M'ra warned her of when she said she'd gain powers after collecting the last passport? She bore a passport to each realm on her chest. As bad as they hurt when they inked, the pain she felt with them was minute in comparison to the crippling weight on her now. "Do you see it?"

"See what?" Rosette asked, her voice shaking.

A muffle of voices Terra couldn't decipher flowed into her ears and two arms collected her and held her like a baby. She opened her eyes, not realizing she'd closed them, and stared into a pair of familiar, yet unfamiliar, eyes.

She woke on the couch in the trella, which was the elfin word for a log cabin as far as Terra could tell. The soft fabric beneath her, she rolled into the pillow behind her head, unsure what happened.

"Are you feeling better?" asked a male voice that sounded as if it was hovering above her.

She turned toward it and blinked. A thick dark-bearded man stared down at her. She sat up, suddenly alarmed, and stared wide-eyed at the elf. His pointed ear tips visible through the long, dark hair on his head woven into a braid. He wore the longest beard she'd ever seen. It hung from his face and stretched to his knees.

She swallowed. "Where's Rosette?" Every bone and nerve in her body suddenly tense.

"Calm down," he reassured her in a sincere voice, meant to soothe her nerves.

Something about him made every hair on her body hackle like a cat. "Where's Clyde?"

Upon hearing his name, Clyde's masked face peered at her over the top of the couch cushions. Terra let out a breath she didn't know she was holding, and opened her arms to the ferret, who crawled into her lap and sat. He wasn't a lap ferret. She didn't think there was such a thing. His little head moved in the direction of the man and his little body tensed. It was as if he was protecting her.

"I'm Kelon. You fainted. I carried you home." His voice soft and reassuring, but there was something odd about him. On the other hand, it seemed she'd met him before.

She studied him for a moment, attempting to figure out what was so off about him. He clearly looked like any elf. No. No, he didn't. It hadn't hit her until that moment. She studied his eyes. They went from jade to shades of blue and back to jade. She'd never seen an elf with hazel eyes; shades of blue and occasionally green like her friend, Nalysse, but never hazel, unless he was a hybrid. "I'm fine. You can go now."

His brows lowered in confusion at her hostile words. "Your reputation precedes you."

What was that supposed to mean? She rolled her eyes and pulled Clyde to her chest. "Seriously, you can go. The door is over there." She pointed.

He raked a hand from mouth to chest through his massive beard and pinched his face. "I should wait for your aunt."

"Suit yourself," Terra snapped, keeping an eye on him. Her mind rolling over what was off until she figured it out. His energy wasn't smooth like the cat's purr of Aradia, but more tense, like a rubber band being stretched. Elves generally radiated a similar energy to their realm. His energy was in conflict with the realm.

His mannerisms ate at her brain. They were familiar; how he raked his hand through his beard and peered at her from under the loose strands of hair on his face, yet she couldn't place him and was positive she didn't remember meeting him.

"We have to go," Rosette's firm voice interrupted the friction in the room. As if she felt it too, she halted in the entry way from the hall to the family room. Her eyes shifting from Terra to Kelon. "The realms have been breached."

Her words took a moment to sink in as Terra's mind connected the dots. That's what she felt! Terra glanced at Kelon for his reaction. It didn't convince her, as he cupped his hands over his mouth in mock surprise and, for a brief moment, his form appeared to shift like static. Terra blinked her eyes, then continued her visual exam of Kelon, noting he now looked quite normal.

3

The prey subspecies relied on cunning not brute strength, and for elves that cunning was related to their communication with plants. Terra was only in the beginning stages of learning to communicate with them as she opened her mind to hear their whispers. Rosette was tight lipped and wouldn't say a word.

Telepathic chatter filled the airwaves as an unintelligible language. Clearing the clutter, she sent a message to a bush as she brushed her hand against it. It didn't respond in words, but a feeling overpowered her and rested in her gut. Those in Aradia were hiding as elves and hadn't moved further than the border.

The invaders wouldn't know elves' ability to communicate with their surroundings, so that was an advantage. She brushed her palm along the top of another bush as she and Rosette, along with other elves, made their way to the transport. *What do they want?*

It took a moment before the response came. Like the last bush, it came as more of a sense of knowledge. The reason was unknown but the plants wouldn't allow the invaders past the border. It wasn't a secret in the realms as there were plenty of stories from the great war depicting the damage plants' roots and vines could do, such as strangle and bury, and tall branches pulling dragons from the sky, but commoners wouldn't know any of that.

She had so many more questions, but all would have to wait as they entered the transport station. Elfin soldiers with bows on their backs and swords sheathed against their legs directed them to a line. Dressed in green cargo pants, matching shirts, and hefty boots, she smiled at one as she walked past. He barely batted an eye.

Terra stepped into the transport, giving a glance over her shoulder as more elves filtered into the station. Elves didn't drive vehicles. They travelled using the transport. A train something like a subway but above ground. It travelled at high speeds and took only moments to get from one spot to another. She stuffed her bag under the seat and set Clyde in his red fabric carrier on the floor in front of her. She hated that he was trapped, but that was the only way for animals to travel the transport.

Rosette stuffed her bag under the seat beside Terra and sat. She wouldn't get anything out of her here. She was tight lipped about tribunal business. Curiosity nipped at Terra. She'd felt shifts in the energy and saw the veil in Aradia nearly split apart as lightning shot across it.

A whooshing sound filled Terra's ears, telling her the transport was ready to move. With a soft jolt it left the station and Terra gasped as all she could see before the transport hit high speed were elves on their journey. Parents and children with no more than a suitcase between them. She wiped a tear that streaked her cheek as an unexpected sadness filled her up.

Even seeing the veil rip open in front of her, she'd given Rosette a hard time. As much as she hated Provence there were worse things. The elves lined up for the transport put life in perspective.

Her mind spun in circles as it tried to understand why the commoners, vampires, and werewolves she was sure, would come to

Aradia. What could the elves possibly have that would be helpful to them? *Were they short on healing salves or remedies? Were they lacking fine elfin fabrics in their life?*

On her trip to Lols, they uncovered the vampire and werewolf underworld and she could absolutely understand if they breeched Canida or Drakonia, especially since Drakonia had one of theirs, but Aradia... Thinking about it was making her head hurt.

Once they reached the station it was a short walk to the curtain. They were in the middle of a decent-sized group filled with families and small children. A little girl ahead of her smiled over her father's shoulder then covered her face with her hands and peeked at Terra through her fingers. Terra pulled her lips together making fish lips. The girl chuckled between her fingers then pulled them away and pushed her lips together. Not quite fish lips, but it was cute and Terra laughed at her.

Rosette nearly snapped her neck when she turned to the side and flashed Terra a "shape up" glance. *Whatever.* She smiled at the girl who was still trying to make fish lips.

As they neared the curtain, she noted elfin guards posted on either side. Usually subspecies came and went from Provence to their realm without notice. The curtain never had guards. She stepped toward the side and watched, noting they were checking passports. *Uh oh!*

It wasn't a secret she was a hybrid, but she had a passport for each realm. That wasn't common knowledge. She stepped back into line and edged toward Rosette and whispered, "They're checking passports."

Rosette's tiny lips pulled into a grimaced smile as she spoke quietly through gritted teeth, "I've got it covered. Keep your mouth closed."

4

Provence City looked smaller as it was filled with more people, and more continued to pass through the curtains. School was cancelled and all students sent to other locations within Provence. Many of the students had parents or relatives on the tribunal and were sent to stay with them. The dorms and every part of the school was used to house the refugees pouring in from the realms.

Terra waited in line with other students to gain access to their rooms in order to get their belongings. Getting through the curtain wasn't as much of a close call as Terra thought it would be. Rosette, as a seated member of the tribunal, wasn't checked for her passport. She was needed immediately, and they gave Terra a free pass. For once she was glad she listened to Rosette. She wasn't always horrible.

There were two lines; one for students and one for refugees waiting for a temporary housing assignment. That line moved slow but Terra's line with other students moved quickly.

Families from all realms, but mostly the lower realms and prey subspecies of elves, fae, and troll, waited for entrance to their temporary homes. She thought of their inconvenience in having to upend their lives in order to come to Provence City. Most of them had never been here in their lives.

Why were the commoners here? Rosette hadn't divulged much, as she was bound to the tribunal. A job she took seriously. Terra was able to figure out by looking at those pouring through that three realms, at least, were breached. She wasn't sure about the higher realms since she didn't see bunches of lycans, dragons, vampires, or harvesters flooding into Provence.

Annoyed at having to be locked into Provence City, she hadn't given the whole situation a lot of thought. The one place in all the realms, with the exception of Drakonia, she didn't want to be. Heck, at this point she might rather be in Drakonia with its metallic odor stemming from Blood River that wound its way through the realm providing needed sustenance for vampires. With its dry desert air and light sandy desolate land, it was ugly to her but was seeming better every moment she waited for entrance to her room.

Vampires were the one subspecies not confined to their realm or Provence City. Those who portalled could use level 3 magic and portal from Drakonia into Lols. Only levels 1 and 2 magic were allowed in Provence City.

Finally her turn, she took in the school with different eyes. The fountain with a back to back lycan and dragon spewing fresh water from their mouths was a sign of peace between the realms. She'd never understood the fountain before but now it seemed obvious. The pickaxe handles on the front doors a bold statement for the harvesters in Thraves, the blue eternal tear drop flowers that vined the staircase were a piece of Aradia. The gemstones embedded in the banister a reminder of the troll realm of Verboten, the infinity door handles a welcome memento to vampires that they too are an integral part of the realms. Last was the sparkly lavender paint that was an exact match to the lavender seas that covered Navarin.

Provence City was more than she'd thought. It wasn't simply a place everyone was welcome, it was more like a citadel. The curtains were a doorway from a realm to Provence. A single entrance and exit point for each realm and the only way to enter or exit through a curtain was to have blood of that realm and a passport. She thought of hers. Phantom pains crushed her chest. She paused on the stairwell to take a deep breath, reminding herself the pain wasn't real.

Each realm had its own symbol and when they inked it caused great pain. They were something like a tattoo. Once a resident of a realm entered and exited their own realm the design imprinted on their chest. Terra was over wondering why she had eight including Lols. On her mind was how commoners could breech the realms. The veils had cracks but they were cracks, small and unnoticed by everyone except her and a few commoners who'd stumbled upon them.

On her trip into Lols to bring back diplomat commoner members for the tribunal she'd noted the veils but now, after being forced to enter Thraves and the last of all the realms, she could see every crack and feel the moment it was breeched. She'd seen the lightning cover the sky and felt the tug of the veil in Aradia.

Her curiosity intense, she'd figure it out. Entering her dorm, she'd expected to see Halsey her fae roommate but was instead met with two fae who were carefully packing Halsey's things into trunks. They were nearly finished, Halsey's side of the room empty of her stuff. The room looked naked and, for a moment, her heart stung as realization hit her in the gut.

Halsey was the Diama of Navarin; a princess who would one day rule the realm. Of course she wasn't packing her own stuff. She was likely whisked away to an undisclosed location and servant fae sent for her belongings.

The fae stopped for a second as Terra entered the room, then continued their work, ignoring Terra. Halsey the fae-wench as she'd once thought of her had become an ally. She'd come through with the kiosk filled with commoner food for Terra, she'd come through with the key that opened the door to the secret portal to Lols, she'd even used her fae influence and knowledge of the old fae language to follow the ancient book they'd found in the great sea fae Merla's cave to find Merla's Realm Grimoire containing the level 4 magic spell that made the veils between the realms, Provence City, the space between all the realms, and the curtains from Provence into the other realms.

The magic spell was so powerful it took blood sacrifice to make it happen. A willing offering of each realm put an end to the Great War. No one had ever really explained the Great War to her, only that all the realms were fighting one another and

Amber, a hybrid, along with six other hybrids and great magic was used to put an end to the war. She only knew that because she'd found it in an old text in the library at Provence Academy. It was an elf/fae hybrid named Cat who loved reading and spent much time in the library who led her to the text.

Terra ignored the fae, as they ignored her, and opened her closet. It didn't appear disturbed. She pulled down her suitcase and unzipped it. The fae not paying any attention to her she moved the boots on top of the box that contained Merla's Grimoire, the scavenger book she'd found, and the glowing blue/white sphere she'd found in Thraves. Everything was in its place.

Clyde scampered towards the box and Terra dropped the lid. He'd been drawn to the sphere since finding it. It was he who found it when M'ra, the minister of Drakonia, sent Terra into Thraves. She didn't go anywhere without Clyde. He stayed close to the closet and at times scratched on the closet door. Anytime she opened the closet he ran inside and sniffed at the box. She didn't understand the connection or what was special about the glowing sphere.

It wasn't only Clyde drawn to the sphere: it whispered to her, only she didn't understand the words. They were mumbled and quiet. She imagined Clyde heard them too and that's why he was so drawn to it. She emptied her dirty clothes from the trip to Aradia into her suitcase and carefully placed the box into it and zipped it then went about packing the rest of her belongings.

M'ra had coerced her into going to Thraves. Bane, a seedy vampire, worked for M'ra and kidnapped Clyde in order to force Terra's hand. She couldn't allow anything to happen to Clyde and so she went to Thraves, insisting Clyde go with her. When she returned after being in all eight realms her blood was used to save a vampire from Lols who suffered a lycan bite for which there was no known cure. *How did her blood save the vampire?* M'ra didn't divulge how, but did warn her she'd start changing… and she had. She could see the realms in a 3-dimensional image, all the cracks in the veils. The energies of the realms more pronounced. She poked the air with the tip of her pointer finger and watched as small ripples pushed through it and vanished. That was something new.

Terra glanced over her shoulder as the two fae opened the door, two more fae met them in the hallway. The group hoisted the trunks, one fae on each end, and carried them. She imagined they'd rather use fae magic to lower those trunks to the first floor as three flights of stairs would be a nightmare to manage with the large trunks. Level 3 magic wasn't allowed, not only not allowed but not possible in Provence.

Realm Walker

Terra zipped her suitcase, took one last glance at the bare room, sighed and left. Clyde followed along behind her. Since Bane had kidnapped him she'd kept him on his harness outside so he didn't wander far from her. It was her negligence in allowing him to run free that got him caught by Bane.

She glanced down the hallway, toward the door that led to the fourth floor and the secret curtain to Lols. Two large white-haired ice dragons, one male, one female, stood guard. They were tall, sturdily built, with large bones. She longed to see what they looked like in dragon form and for the first time admired their magnificence.

Shivers crept up her spine and the déjà vu of being part of something large, larger than her and everyone else, clutched at her guts as if she had to do something, as if it were up to her to fix everything.

She and Clyde made it to the bottom of the stairs. She glanced into the septagonal room beneath. The seven flags of the realms hanging in honor of what each sacrificed to make Provence possible. Dean Salena stood near the front doors guiding students in and out of the school, her back to Terra as she walked into the room and stood in the center marveling at it as she suddenly realized that everyone had given something, a sacrifice, and their sacrifices would not be in vain, but there was something more.

A force and the voice in the box from the glowing ball spoke louder. Its whispers streaming into her ears finally audible: 'Let me out'. *How?* she thought. What was in the glowing ball? Ice cold frosted over her, interrupted by Dean Salena.

Her expression was one of haste. "What are you doing? You must leave, go to your aunt."

Without an argument, Terra left. Nightfall in Provence happened when the fake sun lowered in the fake sky. It wasn't an illusion but something created with magic beyond anything Terra could imagine. She turned the corner onto the road leading to her street and noted Kinzo and Nalysse on the porch swing outside his home.

Weeks ago she'd avoided them as she was new to Provence and hadn't wanted to interrupt. Now she didn't mind interrupting and was happy to see familiar faces. When she approached, she noted the tension between them. The energy like a rubber band about to snap.

Whatever was happening between them was between them and none of her business, but what was happening in the realms was all of their business. She met their surprised gazes as she walked up the steps to the porch, interrupting their heated conversation. Nalysse immediately glanced downward as if ashamed of something. She'd been acting odd towards Terra since they returned from Lols and the tension between her and Kinzo had only grown.

Without poking at their relationship problems, she asked, "What do you know?" Both had parents, like Rosette, who were tribunal diplomats.

Kinzo kept his eyes on Terra, not glancing toward Nalysse who continued to stare at the ground. "The veil was breeched, and commoners have spilled into Navarin, Verboten, and Aradia."

Three realms? She'd thought it was four. "I've been thinking as I packed my room and walked from the Academy. There are guards posted along the curtain into and out of Aradia and every other realm. We crossed the ones in Aradia. Two ice dragons are posted to the door at the school leading to the entrance to Lols. Something big is happening and I felt the veil in Aradia open and saw lightning spread across the sky. I don't understand my connection to magic, only that I can see and feel the veils as if they are a part of me. Somehow, I can manipulate energy as it's all part of me or I'm part of it." She didn't mention her dream. That was probably her hybrid senses and connection to the veils.

5

It was a realization Terra finally admitted to herself, at the same time as out loud. Naylsse lifted her eyes, her expression one of shame. "I stopped at your house but you weren't home. Rosette said you were at the school. We all packed up earlier. I…" She glanced to Kinzo who didn't acknowledge it.

"When we went to Lols, to your house, I found something there. I shouldn't have taken it. It wasn't mine to take but I was," she let out a deep breath, "jealous of the time you were spending with Kinzo. It's not in an elf's nature to keep secrets. I'm sorry."

She opened a satchel resting against the porch swing she sat on.

Kinzo stood, resting his back against the side of the house. Nalysse pulled out a journal. Terra recognized it from the night before she was sent to live with Rosette when she was still at her home in San Francisco. She and her best friend, and across the street neighbor, Noah, accidently found the book. On the cover were the words 'The Origin'. That night they drank her father's alcohol, got drunk, and passed out in his office. Everything went haywire after, and she was sent to Provence City.

Noah returned to her home after she left and read the journal, then it disappeared. Nalysse – she'd found it, taken it. Terra took the book from Nalysse, its cover old but soft in her hands. Kinzo had known. His eyes drifted to Nalysse and narrowed. That was the tension between them.

"Thank you," Terra said. "Listen, you may have been a bit right to be jealous. There's nothing between Kinzo and me but I did take him everywhere with me and he willingly went." She was being a bit harsh, but Terra felt he needed to take some responsibility.

It was true nothing ever happened between Terra and Kinzo, but she'd always been attracted to him and he her. She'd brought him along on her excursions in Lols knowing Nalysse wasn't taking it well. He'd gone willingly and had given Nalysse the cold shoulder when she expressed her feelings. He needed to own up to his own faults. She and Nalysse had admitted theirs, now it was his turn.

Kinzo shifted nervously, as if being confronted by two females was more than he could handle. "I could forgive the jealousy, but not the lie and stealing. Elves don't behave that way, it's shameful."

Terra hadn't wanted to be part of their problem, but she was and he was treating Nalysse wrong, not admitting his own fault. He too was attracted to Terra. She narrowed her eyes and stared hard at Kinzo then turned to Nalysse. "I think we're done here. Will you walk with me?"

She didn't feel any anger towards her. Nalysse offered a weak smile as they left Kinzo on the porch. "I'm really, really sorry," Nalysse offered again, as if she couldn't apologize enough. "What's in that journal you need to read? I think that's why your father had it. Promise me you'll read it."

"I owe you an apology too. We're teenagers and we act like them. I think you deserve better than Kinzo. He knew what he was doing going with me. I didn't need him. I'm the only one of us from Lols. I can handle myself. He went because he wanted to." It was all true. It was also true she'd fallen for

Tania, the harvester hybrid who'd dropped into Drakonia as a harvesting job went wrong. As a seventeen-year-old she didn't only have eyes for Tania who she helped return to Lols.

Tania's job as a harvester hybrid was important and relationships between realms weren't feasible, even for Terra who could enter and exit any realm. There was too much distance between them. They reached Rosette's home.

"You're probably right, but Kinzo and I have been together for so long. I can't imagine not being with him."

Terra imagined how she felt the day her dad died. The grief was overwhelming and she imagined Nalysse felt at least a touch of the grief she had, losing someone you love who is a huge part of your everyday life was devastating. "It's never easy."

Terra did something she thought she'd never do and folded her arms around Nalysse, who returned the gesture.

When she opened the door to Rosette's home she was surprised to see three harvesters in the living room.

6

Afamily of four. A girl about 13 or 14, a baby, and their parents. As Rosette explained they would be staying with them until the emergency was over and it was safe to return to Thraves, Terra wondered how Rosette would weather two teens in the house as she could barely handle Terra. A baby would certainly wake in the night.

Those from the higher lands were all tall. The harvesters, she noted, were like dragons and lycans: tall. But, unlike the lycans, they weren't notably muscular and, unlike the dragons, not large-boned. The father had a notable 5 o'clock shadow. She remembered that most harvester male members on the tribunal had thick facial hair of some kind. Metford, the one who was kicked off for deceiving the tribunal along with the vampire Bane, had a long goatee. All their eyes swirled. Meesha said that allowed them to see spirits. There weren't many harvesters in Provence, only the ones on the tribunal and their families, and not many attended Provence Academy, but the family in Rosette's living room came from Thraves as all tribunal members had homes provided for them in Provence.

Dinner was interesting as there was an uncomfortable silence and nobody ate the same thing. Terra enjoyed oven baked chicken nuggets and fries, while Rosette had some sort of elfin veggie leaf wrap, and the harvesters ate a healthy diet of meat and veggies from their homeland.

She guessed they were omnivores like her, unlike others in the highlands, as lycans and dragons were carnivores. Canida, home of the lycans, was more like midlands and prairies but Sier was highlands where dragons lived inside the mountains. They were strong, powerful, and proud. Did they stay to fight? And why were the harvesters here? They also lived in the mountains. It seemed that would be easier to defend and, if war was happening, wouldn't there be lives to harvest?

She doubted she would get the answers from anyone.

After dinner, she retired to her room to find the teenage daughter was rooming with her.

Terra stared at the fold down bed Rosette asked her to make up for Gillian, the harvester teen. The mattress was thin and the wood rails would be felt through it.

Gillian entered the room after her. "I can do that."

"No." She glanced at her large bed. She felt bad for the girl estranged from her home. Had she ever been to Provence City? "My bed is big enough for the both of us if you'd rather."

The girl smiled, a small dimple popped on her left cheek. She nodded her head. "What is he?" she asked, as Clyde jumped on Terra's backpack that still contained the box with the glowing blue ball, Merla's Grimoire, and the book with the map to where the grimoire was hidden, and now the journal was in her bag too. "He's a black footed ferret. His name is Clyde."

She pushed the bag toward her closet, lifted Clyde off and closed the door.

"Is this your first time to Provence?"

The girl nodded. "It's exciting. I never thought I'd get to come but here we are."

Terra thought about that. The girl probably heard talk about Provence her whole life. It was the center of all the realms, geographically, and the tribunal met here. It was the capitol and contained Provence Hall where the tribunal met and Provence Academy. A school anyone from any realm could attend. Maybe she imagined coming here and attending the school. "There aren't many harvesters around here. I'm surprised that your family is here." She was hoping to get information from the girl.

"I was surprised too."

That wasn't what Terra wanted to hear, but she was only a kid. Why would her parents tell her anything?

The baby whimpered as someone came down the hallway and went into the extra room. She guessed the parents and baby were staying there. The baby!

"Is it your little brother?"

Gillian gave her an awkward glance.

"Is he why your family is here?" It made sense to Terra to protect the children and families of the young.

The girl shrugged.

The fake sun was gone and the fake sky was dark. Tiny lights twinkled like stars and the moon, fake or real, shone above them. The moon, Terra decided, was real, remembering how Kinzo showed it to her when they first met, explaining how it reflected pink over Drakonia when it was in line over Aradia.

She took the journal from her backpack and quickly closed the closet door before Clyde got in.

"He likes your backpack?" Gillian noted with a chuckle.

"He does. I keep treats in there for him," Terra lied. "I'm going to read so I can stay ahead in my classes while the school is closed but I'll turn the lamp on so you can sleep."

Terra dropped back onto the plush bench in front of the window and Gillian climbed into her bed.

Terra opened the journal. An entire story came to life of an elf about Terra's age named Marya. In the year 900, she left the Meridan woods on an adventure, more of a mission with her best friend, to stop the Great War. Her first obstacle: the darklands. Remembering how she'd spotted them in Aradia and how Rosette spoke of them. A place surrounded in spiked trees and sticky brambles. Inside was a darkland and strange creatures.

When she finally finished the story, a mix of anger, betrayal, and shock swirled in her head. Her eyes had other ideas besides waking Rosette up and demanding she explain. When Nalysse told her she had to read it she understood why and what she was. Terra wasn't like any other subspecies. Her kind was created from level 4 magic. It was the only explanation for her ability to enter all the realms. It all started to make sense as her tired eyes drifted to sleep.

7

Terra awoke on the bench. Clyde wasn't in her face as usual but the harvester girl, Gillian, stared at her with wide swirling color in her eyes, her face horrified.

"Why do you have that?"

What? Terra was confused. The journal on her mind, and Marya, and what she learned from the journal. Her anger overtaking her shock, she sat up and jumped off the bench when she noted the closet door open and her backpack in the middle of her floor. "That's none of your business." She rushed to the box the girl had taken from her backpack. That was hers, she had no right.

She'd even been nice enough, feeling bad for the displaced girl, and let her sleep in her bed.

"I'm a harvester and that's a pure soul. Yes, it's my business. You see how it glows blue. It has great power over magic. Why do you have it?"

What? She hadn't known what it was. It spoke to her. It's whispers growing louder and more defined, 'release me'. "Do you hear it?" Terra asked.

Gillian nodded. "Of course I do. You can't keep it, you have to send it to Tranquility."

"I can't," Terra explained. "I don't know why but it wanted me to find it. It talks to me too." She reached for the girl's arms and pulled her downward. She sat on the other side of the box. "You said it was a pure soul, so it's a good soul. Is it possible to release it?"

The girl knitted her brows. "You can't bring the dead to life. The soul belongs in Tranquility with all the other dead pure souls."

She hadn't thought of bringing it to life, only releasing it as it asked. Terra squeezed the girl's hand. "You can't say anything."

The girl's mouth moved, but words didn't escape at first. "I can't. How did you do that?" The girl jumped to her feet then turned on her heel and ran out of the room.

It took Terra a moment to realize what had happened. She'd magically stopped the girl from saying anything. It was something new. She couldn't hide her smirk at what she'd done even if it freaked the girl out.

She placed the box into her backpack and laid it on the bench while she got dressed and brushed her teeth. There were more immediate things she needed to take care of. Marching down the stairs, she found Rosette outside on the patio made with gemstones and brick watering her plants.

She slid the door open, catching Rosette's attention as she spun around, a watering can in her hand.

Terra kept her voice low and controlled since there were so many in Provence and harvesters in their home. Her anger wasn't something she could hide. "You lied about everything: me, my parents, why I'm here. Why am I here?"

Rosette didn't appear shocked. Her expression one of guilt followed by sudden confusion. She clearly knew she'd lied, but not how Terra knew.

"I have something that I think belongs to you, passed down from Marya."

Rosette's eyes widened as she understood. "How do you have that?"

"It doesn't matter. You lied!" Terra seethed, her voice rising an octave.

Rosette put the watering can down and glanced around. "Not here. There are too many ears, and some quite sensitive, but I know somewhere."

Terra, with Clyde in his harness, followed Rosette to the cave. She brought her backpack as she didn't trust the girl. When Tania fell through the veil they hid her the first night in the cave. It wasn't big but it was private. Rosette didn't stop when she entered the cave but went in further until they came to a wall. She pressed her hand against it. Her handprint glowed as a light scanned over her. The wall moved. She turned to Terra. "In here. This is our last resort. A place the tribunal created in the event Provence was ever breached or under attack. There are no cameras or listening devices. We can talk freely."

The walls thick metal, not earth or rock. They were formed by trolls.

"You're right. I've lied, but it was to protect you until you could control magic. You have great command. Your mother and I did grow up together and I covered for her when she and your father escaped. She was 40 weeks pregnant. I helped her hide that. Things weren't good at the time. They would have killed her and you. I always assumed she'd taken Marya's journal with her so you could learn who and what you are. She went to Lols, where she had you, and returned. Your kind was cleansed from the realms. Their immediate families banished to Lols. If she hadn't come back she would have been hunted, you would have been found. I had to help save you."

"I am a realm walker?" On some level last night, after reading the journal, she knew that, but hearing it and processing it were two different things. Her mother saved her from the cleansing, ensuring a realm walker would exist into another generation. The hair on her arms prickled.

"You are, and the last. You must learn how to command magic. You are our only hope."

"I'm seventeen.... What do you mean 'only hope'?" Why should she even believe her? The thought earlier of how she had a destiny; something only she could do, returned. Her gut clenched.

"They've come with an army of wolves, vampires, and warlocks through portals and the veil. Realm walkers were created to keep peace and did so for centuries. It's a new day and time for the return of the realm walker; one who can walk all the realms, mend the veils, and push the commoners back into Lols, but you must first learn to manipulate magic. There are underground tunnels that run to each realm from here. You must go to Drakonia and see M'ra. She is the only one alive who can teach you."

REALM WALKER

Terra's mind swirled like a harvester's eyes, only in confusion. The weight of destiny hanging from her shoulders, heavier than the backpack. Why M'ra? Why any of this? Why couldn't people get along?! She swallowed hard as her throat dried. Tension mounting inside her.

Rosette walked to the wall and pressed her hand. The wall glowed and light passed over her body. "This will take you to Drakonia. You won't need me to get back. Your command of magic will return you when you're ready."

Whatever she had to do, whatever she was, she had something of Rosette's. Terra opened her pack and took out Marya's journal. She handed it to Rosette.

With a tight-lipped smile and a thank you in her eyes, Rosette took the book and folded it under her arm. "Quickly. You must go before the door closes."

Rosette opened her palm. "I need your comicay. I doubt anyone will know you're missing with all the chaos but, just in case, I can confuse them so they won't find you."

That was an admission to Terra that comicays were used for tracking, as she'd always thought.

8

Once the door between Terra and Rosette closed the tunnel became very dark. She couldn't see her hand in front of her face. She reached her hand around her side and fumbled with the pocket of her backpack in search of her cell phone.

It didn't make calls in Provence, or any of the realms other than Lols but it had proved to have many other uses. She grasped the top and pulled it out but it slipped from her hand and crashed to the ground. *Great! I broke another phone.*

The thought instantly reminded her of her father. He tried everything to save her phones from death and she'd done so well with this one. She leaned down and felt along the ground. A furry bundle nudged her hand. Clyde. She reached to pet him and her hand pushed against something cold and hard. Her cell phone. She pressed the button on the side and the screen lit.

A crack ran across the screen but it still worked. She relaxed and turned on the flashlight. The ground and walls were cut from stone. Remembering Marya's journal she called The Origin; Marya and her friend Davi cut through the darklands. They were told to follow the path, not look to the right nor the left or glance behind them. In the dark tunnel she thought it good advice.

The glowing ball's energy warm on her back as heat moved through the backpack. She and Clyde weren't alone. They carried a pure soul. Who, she couldn't even imagine. Someone lost, like Tania had been, a harvesting gone bad. The soul lost in Thraves at the bottom, under the falls for years, waiting to be found.

She talked to the ball and Clyde to break the eerie silence. Fear wasn't an emotion she felt often, but in the dark tunnel it dared to creep into her own soul if she didn't keep her mind busy. "Who are you? Were you there waiting for me? Clyde? Or anyone to find you?"

It stayed quiet and she wished it would whisper to her. Clyde's little feet scampered along, making tiny sounds as they did. Besides his footsteps and her own voice it was silent. She didn't figure the tunnel could be too long as the cave wasn't far from Drakonia. Nothing was far away in Provence. Her mind worked overtime to keep her anxiety low as she walked through the darkness.

"I can feel your warmth. I'd like to know more about you. You don't have to tell me, but it might help. Maybe you could tell me how to release you and why? Why wouldn't you rather go to Tranquility?" Silence persisted. Darn, if the glowing ball suddenly decided to stop talking...

She held the phone in front of her all the way until its glow illuminated a wall. A door, like the one she entered from. Rosette opened it for her. How would she get out? Was she stuck? Was it a trick? She didn't have her comicay. She shouldn't have trusted Rosette. The story about her mom probably another lie. She sat on the rocky ground and stared at the wall.

Clyde ran towards it and scratched as if wanting what was on the other side. Would it work like the curtains into the realms and open for her? She pressed a hand against it. Its familiarity told her Drakonia was on the other side. Holding the flashlight with one hand and pressing against the wall with the other, she watched as her hand moved through the rock.

She pulled it back quick and scooted backwards on her butt. "Impossible. I'm seeing things. Hands don't go through rock. Do they, Clyde?"

He jumped onto her lap and chittered, as if telling her something, and the pure soul whispered. Its words clear and concise: "You can go through it. You have to imagine it in your mind."

It was about time it spoke. She stuffed the cell phone in her pocket and pushed against the wall with both hands. She couldn't see, but she could feel they'd gone through. The rock was like jelly as she pushed forward. Taking a deep breath, she forced her head and body into the rock. Its energy heated and vibrated against her, yet it wasn't hot.

As she pulled her legs through, Clyde scampered between them, his harness around her arm, and they entered a cave. The metallic scent she hated about Drakonia hit her nose. It had become less disgusting as her sense of smell had gotten used to it, but it still caused her to wrinkle her nose.

They were in another cave and soft light shone from around a corner. They followed it until she came to the exit. There was nothing but desert. She couldn't even see the tower on the horizon. They hadn't walked that long and couldn't be too far into Drakonia.

In every direction, the wasteland spread out in front of them. She didn't know which way to go, then she thought of something else. Bane. He was always lurking like he was following her. Surely he'd know where she was. "Bane!" she called.

"Someone showed you the tunnel. Clever. How did you get to this side? It's more than three feet thick."

She whipped around to see the teal blue of the portal vanish behind him. Of course he knew of the tunnel. At one time he was a tribunal diplomat before getting kicked off. His hair slicked, not a strand out of place. His suit not a wrinkle and shoes shined. "I need to see M'ra," she demanded.

He chuckled. "You need to see her? You should have stayed in Provence. She's a busy woman protecting her realm from invaders." He opened the portal.

She pressed her arms over her chest. "She'll want to see me."

He held out a hand. "I don't understand why, but she will. Go, that portal will take you to her."

9

The teal light of the portal vanished and she was in a room in the tower. It looked like the same room from last time, with its warm colors and view of the realm. She was high in the tower. The crimson sky spread across the barren land.

A holographic image appeared. M'ra. The veil covering her face. "Why are you here?"

That was a stupid question. M'ra knew very well why she was there. If anything, she'd planned it. The warning she gave her after sending her to Thraves was grave and had stuck with Terra since, as strange things had started happening like her boiling hot chocolate, climbing through solid rock, forcing Gillian's words to not come out. "Why won't you come in the room in person?"

M'ra, under the dark veil, studied Terra's face. Even through the holocall Terra felt her eyes on her. "The changes have started, haven't they?"

Of course! She knew it! "I crawled through solid rock. I'd say strange things are happening. How did you know any of this?" Terra's voice rising in frustration and anger.

"How did you get here?"

They could play the question game all day. It was Rosette who insisted she go to M'ra, insisting she was the only one who could help her. Marya's journal, that was it! "You're Amber, aren't you? That's why you hide. Show me your face!" Amber, the hybrid she'd read about in the book from the library at the academy. The same Amber who was made, with six other hybrids, into realm walkers. She was mute and couldn't say her name properly, calling herself Emra. Her mind connected the dots: Emra for Amber and now pronounced M'ra. It was her friend Hyacinth who told her that, when starting their second life, they chose their first name.

A teal light flashed behind Terra. When it vanished M'ra in person stood before her. She lifted her veil and pulled it off her head, exposing who she really was. M'ra had shown Terra her face in the past but she'd hadn't known of realm walkers then. She'd been hiding for centuries. Her colorful hair that blended with the room, her hazel-ish eyes like Terra's and her olive skin that, like her hair and eyes, blended with the room. "How do you know of Marya?"

"A journal she called The Origin. My father had it and I found it." She left a lot out but figured fewer details was better. No need to involve others.

"I never saw her again and didn't know she put her story onto paper."

"It passed for centuries from one generation to the next. I don't know how my father had it, but I know why. It was to one day tell me who I am, where I come from, and my purpose."

M'ra's face sullen, her words gentle. "I may look like you, but I'm no longer like you. I have lived many lives and this one is my last. No one needs to live for two millennia. Anyone who knew who I was is dead. You are the one I've waited for. I hadn't given up that you existed. I can teach you, but I can't do all that I used to."

Her words eased Terra's tensions. She didn't lie, or even attempt to. She showed Terra her true self. M'ra sat on the couch inviting Terra to do the same. "There's a lot to tell you." M'ra's voice gentle and kind.

Terra took a seat on the other end of the couch, an expectant expression on her face. Finally, she was getting some answers that were honest. She wasn't a hybrid, she was far more, and one of the very first realm walkers was sitting two feet from her. She had so many questions but they were cycling in her brain so fast she couldn't catch them.

"My family was brought to Drakonia and invited to stay there. When Merla spelled us, she asked for one hybrid from each realm. I stood for Drakonia and came back to the realm with my family. I was their realm walker. When my first life passed of natural causes related to old age I was given a choice of dying or taking a second life. The Minister was old, he'd lived many centuries and was ready to pass on the realm. He offered it to me as the person who'd kept the peace for many years." She paused. "The passing of one Minister to another isn't that simple. He chose me because the ring chose me." She lifted her hand, exposing a ring with a large ruby stone. "I accepted the offer and took the name M'ra. It was a reminder of who I was before I was changed."

It was a sobering story but she wanted to know more about what she was. "Tell me more about being a realm walker."

Realm Walker

M'ra's eyes lit up but her expression was grave as the question elicited both excitement and sorrow. She explained. They were created to keep the peace between the realms and could walk among them all. As the first, they had a lot to learn on their own with only each other to guide the discoveries of their powers. They stayed mostly within their own realms, but each time they left their realm and entered and exited another they bore a mark they named passports.

M'ra showed Terra hers and explained what everything meant. The symbol for each realm Terra understood, but the circles had confused her. The outside circle meant Lols, which Terra already knew, but M'ra explained it means the realms are a part of Lols and Lols a part of the realms. A barrier exists between them. One made long ago. The inner circle meant Provence. A place for all the inner realms, not meant for commoners from Lols. An inner sanctum or, as Terra thought of it, a Citadel. Terra hadn't been wrong.

"My job is to be a peacekeeper?"

"Your job is so much more. It's all on your shoulders as the only realm walker in existence. There were seven of us, but there's only one of you. You will have to use your clever brain and learn to command magic. Realm walkers have incredible control of matter and energy, that's how you crawled through rock." There was something in M'ra's tone that hinted she was holding back. Yet her expression didn't give anything away.

That was pretty amazing, almost more amazing than Terra could fathom. But strange things had happened like forcing Gillian's words to evaporate. "I also forced a girl to not say certain words. How did I do that?"

M'ra chuckled. "Sound is energy. You'll get used to it."

"You're telling me I can manipulate all matter and energy?"

M'ra nodded. "Yes. Tomorrow we start. Tonight you eat and rest." She snapped her fingers and a menu appeared.

"I thought you didn't have that magic anymore. How did you do that?"

"I am a hybrid from birth and I'm a very old vampire. There are many things I can still do."

Terra collected the menu from her. All the questions speeding through her brain came together and she had one thing to ask. It was something she'd been curious about since reading The Origin. "How did you go into Merla's sea cave? You live on land and breathe oxygen through lungs, not gills."

M'ra smiled as if that was the last thing she expected Terra or anyone to ask. "I could shift into nearly anything. I made myself a fish and swam beneath the sea with her. Merla wasn't so bad. She was kind to me and angered by the chaos and hate on the ground between the realms. Changing us and creating Provence, the curtains and the veils between the realms were the only answer she could find to save what was left of the realms. She feared, if the war continued, we'd all parish or exodus into Lols."

Terra, still focused on the shifting, didn't think to ask the obvious question why it would be so bad to escape to Lols, asked: "You shifted Marya and Davi into trolls. That's how you hid in Verboten. Why trolls?"

M'ra's knowing smile creased her face. "I could shift myself into almost any living thing, but I could only shift others into trolls."

Ohh! That made so much sense. It was something she'd wondered about since reading The Origin. "Chicken strips, loaded tater tots, and a bowl of strawberries."

M'ra stood. "And to drink?"

She could have anything. "A chocolate shake with whipped cream and chocolate syrup drizzled on top."

"Your food will be here soon."

"One more question," Terra said.

M'ra's brows lifted in curiosity.

"If vampires only drink blood and don't eat food, why do you have the best commoner food in all the realms?"

She chuckled as if the answer was obvious. "We have the best chefs in all the realms and we have commoner visitors from time to time. We want them happy and willing. Their blood is tastier that way and they don't fight us It's a partnership." She winked.

10

erra was almost too excited to eat, but the aroma was so delicious she devoured the breakfast wrap stuffed with sausage, cheese, potatoes, and eggs, and drank every ounce of orange juice in the glass.

M'ra appeared from a teal light with a heavy fur coat and boots in her hands. She herself was dressed in a thick fur, boots to match, and a hat. "These should fit." She handed the coat and boots to Terra.

"Where are we going?" Terra asked as she took the coat and boots, placing the boots on the ground.

"The edge of the world. It's cold, try these on."

The coat fit fine and warm, snug gloves were in the pockets. The boots were a bit large and when Terra took a step they chafed her ankle.

"You can change that," M'ra said, noting the extra room between Terra's heel and the shoe heel as she winced with each step.

Terra lifted a brow. "How?"

"Matter and energy. Imagine them snug and comfortable on your feet and command them."

Terra gave it a thought and imagined the boots fitting comfortably, not riding up her heel with every step. She lifted her foot and the boots clung in place. "I don't understand."

"Matter and energy."

The questions circulating in Terra's mind yesterday were on rapid fire now. Forget the boots. "Have the commoners really invaded?"

M'ra's colorful eyes gave Terra a once over as she replied. "Yes, they have. Vampires, wolves, and something called warlocks in Aradia, Navarin and Verboten."

Hyacinth had done research in chat rooms when they went to Lols. She mentioned the vampires and wolves hated each other. How had that changed in only a few weeks? And what exactly were warlocks? Her human understanding was that warlocks were something like a witch or sorcerer. "Warlocks?"

M'ra lifted Terra's hand and spun her under it as her eye exam continued. "They have a far-reaching control of magic. From what my vampires have seen, they can shift, spell things, and control lightning. It doesn't seem they all do the same thing, but they have banded together."

"Why? What do they want?"

M'ra's face grave, she folded her hands together in front of her. "They haven't made any demands yet, but have attempted to take command of the capitols in Navarin and Verboten. Not with much luck. My vampires also report they are manning the borders between the lands. That's why you need to be ready and we don't know how much damage these warlocks can do."

Not with much luck. What did that mean? "The fae and trolls are unharmed?"

"As of now," M'ra responded without detail. Terra figured she wouldn't get that from anyone, but didn't doubt the Minister was well aware of how their attempts failed. Another question begged Terra's attention. She'd been curious and, like all thoughts in Terra's mind, they didn't follow a logical pattern. "How did you know my blood would heal the vampire?"

"I didn't for sure, but had a hunch. I saved vampires when I was a realm walker. It was something we kept secret. If you were a realm walker then you could heal her, but I needed you to go to Thraves to prove you were who I thought," she responded.

"We have to go," M'ra urged, before Terra had a chance to shoot off another question.

A teal light swallowed them and they landed in a clearing surrounded by snow. A cabin rested at the bottom of the hill they stood on near the tree line. M'ra wore dark glasses, a scarf over her face covering it below the sunglasses, gloves on her hands, and fur clothing. Not a bit of sun could reach her.

"Where are we?" Terra asked as she scanned the snow-covered hill.

"Greenland. It will be nightfall soon, so we need to get started. You already sized your boots so we'll go a little bigger. I want you to pile snow."

Terra eyed her awkwardly and lowered the backpack. Clyde, on his harness, dug into the snow. "How?"

"Like you sized your boots and crawled through rock. Imagine it and order the snow into a pile," M'ra stated, as if it was that easy.

Terra glanced at the feet of snow around them and imagined a heap a few feet from where they stood. Nothing happened at first, but she kept imagining then went back to her earliest lesson when Meesha had her touch the ground and how she began feeling the energy after that. She closed her eyes to block out distractions and let the energy fill her up. The steady heartbeat of Lols pumped within her.

Not letting the mound of snow escape her mind, she opened her eyes and a mound as tall as her stood a few feet from them where she'd imagined it.

"Impressive. You don't go small. Now take the snow and imagine it falling away from the mound."

Terra closed her eyes again, Lols' steady rhythm in beat with hers, but she felt something else this time. The beat skipped like a palpitation. She opened her eyes seeing vaguely the swirling colors of an elevator. When she and her friends came to Lols a few weeks ago, Tania had shown them to her. They were a way to travel around Lols quickly. Once inside the elevator they only needed to imagine where it went and it would take them there.

The elevators had served them well. The only drawback was, once it dropped them off, the elevator didn't stay open and they had to find another permanent one, but they were everywhere… apparently, even at the edge of the world. This one was several feet behind the house at the edge of the clearing.

She refocused her mind, eyes open, and concentrated on the elevator. She imagined the snow flying off the mound towards it. A snow saucer hit the tree nearest the elevator, startling her. She shifted her gaze to the mound and watched the snow literally fly off the mound in snow frisbees, hitting the trees below. She then scanned the tree line and imagined snow frisbees hitting everywhere her eyes saw. It was almost fun.

"Disks. I like it," M'ra noted with a chuckle.

Grumbles erupted from the tree line and Terra spotted several people dressed in heavy fur and covered head to foot like M'ra. Vampires.

"My guards. Maybe you should tone it down a bit."

Terra brought the snow frisbees higher. They crashed into the tops of the trees, snowflakes dropping to the earth.

"It seems you can work matter, but energy is a little different - you can't see it. I want you to build a barrier around us."

A barrier. How did she do that? Energy wasn't something she could really imagine, then she realized it was. Earthquakes and waves in the ocean were energy. It couldn't be seen, but its effects could be. Without asking how, she went with what her gut said and opened her hands, pulling her fingers towards them. She imagined energy flowing towards and surrounding them.

Then, to test it, she sent the snow frisbees towards them. They hurled forward and, before they hit, she ducked. They crashed against the invisible barrier, snow flaking to the white ground.

"Very impressive. You are your father's daughter."

Terra's father. He was a dragon, not a realm walker. In The Origin it outlined that a realm walker could partner with anyone, but their firstborn would always be a realm walker. In her case it was her mother who was a realm walker, not her father. "You mean my mother."

"Hmm…" M'ra said then realized she'd spoken her words out loud. "No, your father. Of course you wouldn't know." Her eyebrows flattened as her face grew grim. "What I'm going to say will be a surprise, but don't think less of the man who raised you because he was your father in every sense except the donation of genetic material."

What was she saying? Terra's mind froze on the 'of course you wouldn't know'. Duh! Everyone had lied to her and now they expected her to "fix" everything. Her, a seventeen-year-old senior in high school, who wanted to go back to her life in San Francisco, to before she knew any of the nonsense of the realms.

Her cheeks went red as anger boiled inside her. "Of course I know nothing! Nobody tells me anything until it slips or someone needs something." She folded her arms over her chest. "Leave me here. I don't need you and certainly don't need to save the realms; what have they done for me or my kind? Whatever happened to realm walkers? Why am I the only one?" Her sudden rage was a build up from the past couple days and hearing the father who raised her wasn't her real father was the final straw.

The energy shield she created erupted and spread in a circle around them, blowing the rest of the mound of snow into the woods as it smashed against the trees. The ripples in the energy seen moving through the air.

M'ra's expression went from grim to impressed then grave as she faced Terra. "You have every reason to be upset. Let's go to the house and I'll explain from the beginning."

11

The cabin was rustic, with wood walls and cozy puffy furniture in fall colors. It wasn't large, but large enough for a family to get away for a weekend.

Terra's true father was a realm walker. His parents were also realm walkers. They could be with anyone except each other, which sounded a bit two-faced. It wasn't because of Merla's spell but was considered taboo since the union of two realm walkers might create something stronger than a realm walker, and it had.

His parents were both realm walkers. His mother of Thraves, and his father of Drakonia. She didn't even need to ask. M'ra explained that her line stayed in Drakonia just as the others stayed in their respective realms, which meant Terra was M'ra's ancestor. When Terra's grandmother became pregnant, she married a harvester before it was learned and birthed a son – Cyrus.

He stayed in Thraves, not knowing for many years that he came from a union of two realm walkers. It wasn't until he was grown that his mother told him the truth. His anger consumed him and he quadrupled the size of Provence and demanded it be a home for realm walkers, that they deserved their own realm and shouldn't be servant to anyone. He started a war for realm walker rights and forced the hand of the realms to comply with his wishes. He used his power to distort realms and crack the veils and created the curtain to Lols in Provence.

Her mom was the realm walker of Aradia. Rosette had a real sister who fell in love with a dragon. Terra's mom, Rosette, and the dragon's best friend helped them keep their relationship a secret until she became pregnant, then they helped them escape into Lols. Terra's mom and his best friend, also a dragon (the father who raised her), became close in those days and she went to Cyrus to plead with him to stop. Instead, she fell in love.

When Terra's mom became pregnant it was kept secret. Cyrus helped hide her and her father, she thought, assisted in getting them out of the realms. Rosette never mentioned Cyrus helping her mother and father escape. Had she left that out on purpose? Had Cyrus not actually helped? Or had Rosette lied? No, her expression had been one of honesty, as was M'ra's. Plenty was concealed in their words and the actions of others. One day it would come full circle.

The leaders of every realm decided the only way to stop the nonsense and bring peace to the realms was to cleanse the realms of all realm walkers. Terra was born in Lols. M'ra always thought she was taken by her father to join his best friend but she didn't know anything for sure. There are many things she knows, but what happens in Lols she knows little of.

She is second generation of a new kind of realm walker. A stronger realm walker. Rosette wouldn't have said anything to preserve her life. If it was known what she was before the time was right, they may have, in fear, cleansed her.

There was only one question pressing on Terra's mind. She only knew her mother through stories from her father. "Why did my mom return to the realms?"

"She had to, to protect you. The last realm walker and her baby."

"And what happened to Cyrus? Was he cleansed?"

"We don't know. He was close to the harvesters but they wouldn't have allowed him to survive the cleansing. He betrayed them. They were angrier than anyone, yet his soul has never been found. That's why Bane did what he did and that's why I trust him."

So much was going through Terra's head, but mostly it was focused on her father not being her father. He raised her as his own, sacrificed his own life for hers. Then a terrible thought overwhelmed her. "My father didn't die in an accident. He was killed because of…" She gulped, unable to say what her mind was thinking.

"You don't know that. Rosette knew where to find you because of her sister. No doubt they found ways to stay in touch, to communicate on some level, even if only through the plants."

That rolled around Terra's head. Had she met her true aunt? Was she friends with her father? It would seem she had to have met her. How else would Rosette know where to find her. All this time she hadn't liked Rosette much but earned a new appreciation for the selfless danger she put herself in to bring Terra to Provence. Terra felt a little better, then a sick feeling crept into her gut. Rosette said the immediate families of the realm walkers were banished to Lols. M'ra's unspoken words said as much as the spoken ones. "You haven't mentioned the families of the realm walkers. Did… Do I…" A lump formed in her throat as she tried to spit the words out.

As if M'ra read her mind, maybe she did, she responded: "An aunt. Many years younger than your father. Cyrus' father eventually had a child, a girl, not much older than you. Under my authority I didn't banish her to Lols but sent her with loving parents. A couple; hybrids in fear of their lives as they thought hybrids would be next. They spent their lives passing as elves but weren't pure blooded. It wasn't a choice. Cyrus never knew about her and she couldn't stay in case anyone else did. She has unique abilities as the hybrid sister of a realm walker with hybrid elfin adopted parents and her connection to vampires."

"She's alive, in Lols?"

"She is very much alive," M'ra responded, innuendos masked in her words. Terra knew better than to even ask. One day she'd find her. She had a true aunt, who was young, not old like Rosette. In the immediate future she needed to understand what this special job was she was to perform and how she would know when and what to do. "When is the right time?"

"Now, Terra. You can purge the realms of the commoners. That will make you a hero in the eyes of the realm leaders. Yes, they will fear you, but they won't harm you.

Merla warned that if realm walkers were ever harmed the realms would crumble. It's happening. Rosette will take care of the tribunal. She is a worthy diplomat."

It was too late. They'd already harmed realm walkers by cleansing them. Certainly, they wouldn't have a problem repeating. It seemed their consciences weren't twisted over it but all that was pre-tribunal. It was almost too much for Terra to process at once. Her whole life was a lie. She was a forbidden child, hidden away, and now expected to save everyone. A strangled sigh escaped her lips as her stomach turned.

M'ra spoke, her words of no comfort: "I need to return to my realm. I will leave my guards in the woods. I want you to stay here. You are safer here, as they are focused on invading the realms not Lols, and they don't know about you. I don't see any way they could. I'll return tomorrow."

12

M'ra hadn't lied. Night fell early. Terra watched from the window, the energy of the elevator calling her. She could so easily go outside and walk right into it and go anywhere in Lols she wanted. She could go home and see Noah, search for her aunt. It gave her comfort to know she had a blood relative alive somewhere with unique abilities.

Her mind not focused on solving the mystery of her aunt yet, but Noah. There was so much to tell him, or she could surprise Tania in New York. Her thoughts lingered on Tania. She'd rather give her a call first since they weren't ever a "thing" really. It was only the start of something. She could have moved on.

A call – that was it. She had her cell phone. No matter what, she always had it. So many times it had saved her even when it didn't make calls. She could call Tania. No, she thought again. Noah, she could call him. He'd read The Origin. He knew the story. She pulled her phone out of her backpack and sighed at the crack in the screen, hoping it still made calls.

A fire crackled in the fireplace as she pulled a large throw pillow off the couch and lay down in front of it. The phone rang a couple times before Noah answered. She was elated to see his face. They always video chatted.

"Why aren't you here?" he asked, meaning in San Francisco.

"I'm in Greenland."

His features distorted in surprise. "What?"

She and Noah could talk candidly about anything. He was her best friend and like a brother. "You remember that book you found? I'm a realm walker."

"Get out of here. No way!"

"Truth."

His face bright as a star with surprise. "What can you do? What are your powers?"

She glanced at the fire and it gave her an idea. She turned the phone around.

"Watch." Instead of pulling energy towards her, she pushed it away. It smacked into the fire and it roared so high she had to duck. The flames licked the stone surrounding the fireplace.

A teal light flashed behind her and she stuffed the phone under the pillow.

M'ra hadn't lied about the vampire guards either. A tall, good looking one with a baby face stared at her. His voice serious, "What was that?"

She shrugged. "I stoked the fire. I guess I'm not real good at it but I'm fine and will leave it alone."

He stared at the flames then tossed on another log. "That should last for the night. No need for you to touch it." His words filled with warning.

"Thanks."

He flashed out and she reached for her phone beneath the pillow.

"Oh my gosh. Who was that? He sounded hot," Noah asked.

"He kind of was. That was a vampire. There's a bunch outside guarding me. That's why I'm here instead of there with you."

"I'm jelly."

"No, you're not."

"If he's as hot as he sounded, yes, I am. Tell me more."

Noah had been her best friend since they were kids. He lived across the street with his mom. She didn't have any problems dropping her life story on him. Everything that happened. She was an open book.

His eyes lit up and he pulled the phone closer to his face. "That's wild. I can't believe my best friend is like the world's savior."

"I'm not, or I don't want to be. I can't even decide what to eat most days, how do I save the world?"

"I know you and you'll find a way. You've always been a leader not a follower." He changed his train of thought. "You control matter and energy like waves."

"Yeah."

"Can you send me a message carried in a sound wave?"

She thought about that. She could at least try. "Plug your ears." She didn't want him to hear it yet. It was a game. He could tell her when he got it.

He did. She glanced away for a second and pressed her face to the ground then said, "I love you, Noah," then imagined the message in Noah's ear. She listened as it floated through the air away from her and smiled. She put her hands on her ears and pulled them away so Noah would know to unplug. "Tell me when you get it."

When they hung up she was left alone with her thoughts and Clyde, who suddenly jumped up from where he'd been lying and raced through the cabin then rolled on the floor towards her. She collected the pillow from the ground and tossed it onto the couch then leaned back on it and turned on the TV. She flipped through the limited selection of channels then noticed the DVD player.

Under the cabinet holding the TV was a small collection of movies. She pushed one in that sounded good and took her place on the couch. Clyde continued his craziness until, finally exhausting himself, stretching his long body on the couch beside her.

She fell asleep but woke when a violet light flashed, followed by two teal lights. Her eyes popped wide open as the vampire from earlier and another faced off with a tall young man. His braids whipped into the air as he spun, avoiding the hands of a vampire. She gulped as his acrobatics kept him just out of the vampires' reach.

M'ra said she could control energy, sound was energy. That's how she'd kept the harvester from talking. If she could do that, maybe she could use that ability to get away now. "Freeze!"

The vampires froze and the braided guy slipped between their frozen grasp towards her. She hadn't meant them. She meant him. There wasn't time to figure out how to unfreeze them as she bolted from the couch jumping over the back, Clyde on her heels, and flung the door open.

The cold air hit her face. Clyde ran ahead of her toward the light, as if he knew exactly what she was thinking. It was that psychic connection she believed they had. The snow wet and cold on her socked feet as she ran towards the woods. Her mind focused, she barely noticed the other vampires shoot out of the woods with wicked speed. Her only goal was to get to the elevator.

The violet light flashed in front of her just as she was about to run into it. She stopped and light wound around her body. M'ra's words 'you control matter and energy' came to mind as she collected the energy with her hands and sent him reeling backwards.

A cord of light wrapped around her middle as the braided man pulled her towards him and warned the vampires: "Don't come any closer."

The cord stemmed into another that wrapped her throat. Matter and energy. Light was energy. The elevator was there. If she could twist the energy, maybe she and Clyde could get away. He stepped closer to the elevator as she used her hands to collect the energy then sent it towards him, but the cord was still around her neck and she and Clyde, who clutched her pant leg, went blasting with him into the elevator.

13

M'ra

How could they possibly lose her? It was seven against one. She'd had the vampire girl who'd been bitten by a lycan and saved by Terra brought to the conference room. She owed them her life and M'ra expected to cash in. "Tell me about the warlocks."

The girl swallowed, her face studying M'ra's through the holocall. Bane by her side. "They have strong magic. Can do many things."

"Like vanish?"

She shrugged. "They have these runes, tattoos that give them special powers. They don't all have the same ones. Some can portal." She thought for a moment. "The gateways. They're like portals, sort of. Warlocks are the only ones that can see them, some warlocks. Maybe all." She twisted in her seat nervously. "They can take you wherever you want."

They traced bloodlines and lineage, had an entire team that worked on the lineage of the original seven realm walkers and the legacy of their immediate families. All twenty-one residing in Lols. She'd had her vampires switch the tribunal's list with the one provided to Terra and her friends went they went to Lols to find the girl and five new tribunal members. It only made sense they use relatives of the seven original realm walkers.

Terra had done one better. Their blood proving they were far more than hybrids, but gateways. In her long life, she hadn't spent much time in Lols. That was to her disadvantage now. "Did the warlocks create them?"

The girl glanced upward at Bane as if nervous in his presence. "No. I don't think so. They just are. It's a mystery, and it was the warlocks that discovered how to travel through them, but they didn't need to create such a thing, as some can could portal anywhere. They've been more useful to vampires and wolves."

M'ra raised an eyebrow as she studied the girl. "Vampires and wolves can't see them."

"No, but with the warlocks' help we have created tools that allows us to track them. They are a disturbance of energy. No one knows where they came from."

M'ra thought about that. How did they know where to find Terra? The girl had told her much, but never mentioned Terra. "Vampires and wolves get along in your world?"

The girl laughed, relaxing for a moment, then straightened her face and tensed her shoulders. "No. We don't get along but we do have a pact, a truce that helps us all to manage living together. Vampires don't work with wolves so it seems they came together to take these realms. I don't know what else they'd want or why they want these realms."

Terra

The lightning cord around her neck, she'd fallen on top of him. She climbed off and took her stance on the opposite side of the space. Only a few feet separated them. For a few minutes they studied each other. His dark eyes burning against her flesh as they moved from her feet to her face.

His broad shoulders, toned arms showing beneath the sleeves of his shirt, strong jaw, and dark skin made it impossible for her to tear her eyes away. She tried but they bounced right back. He was the most beautiful male she'd ever seen. He was even hotter than Kinzo, her elf friend.

Beautiful or not, she didn't like him. "Why did you try and kidnap me?"

His full, kissable upper lip tugged upward in disdain at her accusation. "I wasn't trying to kidnap you. I wanted to talk to you but those vampire guards of yours wanted to kill me."

She folded her arms over her chest. "They aren't *my* guards and they wouldn't have tried to kill you if you hadn't attempted to kidnap me!"

"I wasn't trying to kidnap you!" he said loudly under his breath, his lips barely moving. Next he flung more accusations her way. "Why have you trapped us in here?"

"I haven't! I'm sure it was your weird magic lightning cord thing that did it." She turned her head away from him, her eyes still watching from the corner as they couldn't stop inspecting the eye candy across from her. She didn't think he was entirely wrong as the energy buzzed through her hands. Unwilling to admit to him she may have trapped them but wasn't sure how to untrap them.

"Hank," he announced. His devilishly gorgeous face saying: *if we're going to be trapped together we should at least introduce ourselves.*

That was no name for a god. Ares or Zeus would be more fitting. Her body trembled as she held in the laughter. He did have lightning in his hands and she didn't want it wrapped around her again.

He put a hand up in surrender. "I don't mean you harm."

She folded her hands over her chest in defiance. If he hadn't meant to harm her, why was he after her? M'ra didn't think they'd look for her, and did anyone in Lols even know about her? It seemed they weren't privy to anything the realms did. "You have a strange way of showing that, wrapping an energy cord around my neck. Is choking someone a sign of friendship where you come from?" Her words loaded with bite.

"Of course not. Those vampires..." He paused. "Instead of arguing we need to find a way out of here. We need to work together to get out of this."

Work together! He was right. She released a long sigh. She just needed to figure out how the energy worked so she could get them out of the pickle, but first she wanted answers. Realizing to herself that's why she subconsciously did it. It was her fault. She'd frozen the elevator. The normal rainbow of colors stopped as if time stopped around them. "Why would I work with someone who tried to kill me?"

His face twisted in frustration. "Kidnapping to murder. That's a big jump. I didn't try and do either. You were never in danger, not from me..."

Hidden Passages

Terra didn't agree, but she needed time to figure out a way out of the elevator. She'd frozen the vampires and crawled through rock. Somehow, she could make the elevator work again. The energy vibrated against her palms, reminding her she could harness it if only she knew how. All this stuff about being a realm walker and she didn't have an innate ability to do anything. It seemed to her she should.

He lowered himself to the floor of the elevator and sat cross legged. Clyde sniffed at his foot then jumped backwards when it twitched. "I do owe you an explanation and we need to get out of here for both our sakes. I'm a warlock and I have a guard. She's a powerful soldier. If I'm gone too long, she'll notice and come after me and she'll find me… us."

Now they were getting somewhere. "Keep talking."

He rubbed his hands along his legs, at first not meeting her eyes. "Many millennia ago, the first human was born. Someone with no connection to magic and they populated like mice, spreading like a disease. They feared those with magic if they couldn't use us for their means. They condemned and pushed magical beings to the edge of Earth where they discovered the realms beyond the human realm. It was the fae who discovered the tunnel between the realms. My kind, who come from Marsidia – the inner realm – helped the fae and others escape the human realm until it was realized we couldn't trust the fae and a gateway was created between the middle realms and ours. The fae locked us out of the middle realms – our only path home." He lifted his chin and met her gaze.

Hank's confession sounded as crazy as everything else, meaning it was at least plausible, and she didn't put anything past the fae. Now the warlocks were there in the realms That's why Provence was on lockdown. It was his kind who invaded. She lowered herself and pulled her knees to her chest. "Now they are in the realms. Why don't they just go home?"

"We can't. We need the Stones of Hovrath to unlock the portal between the middle realms and the inner realm of Marsidia."

And if it couldn't get crazier, it just did. Marsidia and special stones. "What are these stones?"

"A key. There are two sets of stones. One set gets us into Marsidia, the other gives us passage out. We need these stones to get home."

This was giving her a headache. "Why would the fae lock you out?"

His face twisted in frustration and it was still mesmerizing to her. "Humans. They figured it out and a war between magical beings and them raged. Those already in the realms left my ancestors behind so the war didn't enter their new world. We had no choice but to hide our true selves and blend with humans."

Terra's mind buzzed with all the secrets she'd learned in such a short time. Level 4 magic created the realm walkers, the veils, curtains, and Provence, but it wasn't the first time it had been used. Merla's grimoire was in her backpack still at the cabin with the glowing soul. The glowing ball: was it Cyrus? M'ra said the harvesters never found him. She refocused on the grimoire. Did Merla modify the spell that originally separated the realms to create more? Sacrifice. Was sacrificing their own to Lols what gave them the power to create a veil?

Realizing he only wanted what she wanted - answers - her heart softened. "I'm Terra." She offered her hand across the short distance between them.

He took her hand and Clyde touched his little nose to their folded hands then placed a front paw over them. It was Clyde's way of telling Terra all was OK. Hank's touch was warm and exciting. It buzzed with energy.

"What are you?" he asked.

"I'm a pissed off teenager."

The tension between them lessening, he smiled at her comment. "You're not an ordinary teenager."

Never a truer statement. She was learning that, for a normal kid, she was anything but normal. Neither was he. She noted a tattoo on his forearm and wondered how many more he had hidden. It was like a secret language in black ink. "What is that?" she asked, pointing to it.

He ran a finger over the tattoo. "It gives me powers." He pulled up his shirt, revealing tight abs and a defined chest. A wave of wanting crossed Terra. In the same place she had a circle and passport for every realm, he had an X. "Our kind was sacrificed so everyone else could live peacefully in the realms without human interference. I was born with this."

Sadness overwhelmed her, and a longing to help him. Not wanting her teenage desires to get the best of her, she needed to know if anything he said was true. There was nothing she didn't put past the fae, yet they weren't all bad. Halsey was a nightmare roommate until she came around. Kayln was a bubblehead and a bit snooty, but also a good friend. "Whatever problems your ancestors had are in the past. The fae who live in the middle realms…" She figured using his terms was best until she knew more, enough to give him some trust. "They aren't the enemy. They aren't responsible for what happened."

"You're right, but not all warlocks see it that way." He stood and offered her a hand.

"If you can help me find the stones my kind can go home."

She accepted his hand, her body bathing in his warmth. "What makes you think I can help you?"

"You're different." Every follicle of hair in his shaven face danced beneath his skin.

The colors of the elevator moved again as they pulled their hands away from each other. She was different. She glanced again at the tattoo on his forearm. The zigzag line reminded her of old fae. She glanced at the book, unable to read it. "The mark on your arm, that gives you power. It's written in a language."

His brows lowered and his dark intense eyes narrowed. "It's a word from our ancestral language. How would you know that?" He became very defensive, proving to Terra that he was familiar with the old fae language.

It didn't really prove anything, other than his kind was fae kind or they were his kind first, but to her it said a lot and she was going to get the book and show him. Not the grimoire, as it was dangerous, but the other. "I'm not so different than you."

"We only want what was taken. It was the Warlocks who found and pioneered the realms," he said in full belief of his words as he shuffled his feet nervously.

If warlocks and fae were mortal enemies, or relatives or whatever it was he was getting at, then helping him might be worth the effort. She doubted it was as simple as he believed. Nothing else was and there were always two sides to a coin.

She didn't know that for sure. Maybe it was the other way around. The one thing she'd learned, and was confirmed every time she learned something new, is that one person's truth wasn't the only truth. "Why the vampires and wolves?"

"We have a truce. That's how we survive without harming one another. We have our lands and keep our peace on Earth. We all have one thing in common and that is to not reveal our true natures to humans. If the vampires and wolves are helping then there is something in it for them." He paused, turning his eyes downward. "I need to get back. I've been gone too long." He raised his eyes and met hers.

She lifted a brow. Was that a threat or a warning? "Do you trust me?" she asked.

"Yes, I do. I can't explain why, but I do."

She felt similar. As much as her heart was telling her to trust him, her brain was yelling for her to check out his story, to find the facts and the truth. On another level that she couldn't explain, she understood that she'd frozen time, although she didn't speak those words to Hank. "Go back and I'll find you."

She needed to get back to M'ra who always had the answers. She was the oldest living being in any realm.

14

The Tribunal

Kierra's red tail plumage stood on end as she raised. Every troll standing with her. "Wolves have taken our capitol city. They stand guard and patrol the streets but haven't penetrated our capitol building. The Mayor has been taken through the tunnels to safety and our guard works on a defense. We are readying our silver tipped arrows, daggers, and bullets. Our dream walkers are on alert as the wolves must sleep at some point. They don't know us, our strengths or our weaknesses. These wolves are uncultured and brutes but haven't harmed a single troll yet, as long as we do as they say."

Maglesh, the troll who always had to put in a word, added to Kierra's statement: "Their numbers are large. They have surrounded the realm and blocked passage into Provence. No more trolls will pass on land, only by tunnel."

As the eldest lycan, Lukas stood, his large frame towering over the trolls. "If they've taken your borders they understand we can't travel from one realm to another." He sucked in a deep breath. His voice forceful: "We will send our best lycans to block the interior border of Provence."

"Without a passport they can't enter Provence," Colton the fire-dragon stated, his words blasting through the morbid silence of Provence Hall.

"We don't think they can, but they aren't lycan. They are something different – a hybrid form – we must do everything to ensure they can't cross into Provence or any other realm. Every realm should be on alert and have their militaries ready," Judge said, his lycan words rang true as each diplomat swallowed hard.

Liam, the eldest fae, stood and all fae diplomats rose with him. "Vampires. They walk in daylight." Wide eyes and hushed whispers went around the room. "They patrol our borders and attempted to portal into our palace. Our strong wards kept them out for now. The diama is safe in Provence but the

King and Queen are trapped in the palace with the guard. We got almost everyone out. Those who remain are prepared to battle."

Ernessa, a testy vampire, stood. "How can they walk in the daylight?"

"A spell of sorts is our guess, which means they act with others who have strong magic. We are mounting an attack using our blood to lure them. In their delirium we are hoping to trap them on Pena Island." Liam studied the faces of the other tribunal members. "Their numbers are many and we may not have enough fae blood." Blood from the pureblooded had an adverse affect on vampires.

"If we offer you supplies of lycan blood and saliva, mixed they may offer the same result as a bite," Lupe, one of the junior lycans and mother of Terra's friend Meesha, suggested.

Lukas, the eldest lycan, agreed.

The dragons and harvesters agreed they could spare.

"We accept the offers, but how do we get the blood to Navarin?" asked the fae Allwyn, Kayln's father.

Rosette stood, straightening her skirt before she spoke. Her goal was to keep them away from Terra. "We use the tunnels under Provence. We can do a blood drive here in Provence City and we, as diplomats, can carry the blood through the tunnels. It is our duty."

Conversation erupted and it was decided Rosette's idea could work since the tunnel in Navarin led to a sea cave. The vampires hadn't entered the seas and, should they, would be met with a strong, poisonous defense. Should the vampires breach the wards, a battle and lycan poisoned blood would be waiting.

The eldest elf rose and the diplomats hushed. "They don't know our weaknesses and strengths. We know theirs. Offense is the best defense in Navarin and Verboten but in Aradia we have a trickier enemy that we know nothing about. They call themselves warlocks."

"How can we help?" Devan, the newest vampire on the tribunal, asked.

All elves stood in support of their eldest and realm. "They hide under cloaks of invisibility and transformation – disguising themselves as elves. The plants have created a barrier, keeping them out of the heart of Aradia. It's held long enough to get people safely to Provence but won't last as they have magic like we've never seen. Beams of lightning and fire comes from their hands. They manipulate with their minds. This is an enemy we don't know."

Liam stood and cleared his throat. "That may not be entirely true. We have carvings under the palace that tell a story we've never understood, of creatures with such magic. If we can interpret the carvings maybe we can find their weakness."

The revelation brought about strong discussion and anger.

"Why have we never heard of this?!" Colton roared.

"They are ancient, drawn before the veils separated us and were taken more as lore than truth," Allwyn stated. Before he was elected to the tribunal and moved his family to Provence he'd worked as a historian. The carvings weren't well known, even among the fae.

Elin, the youngest Harvester on the tribunal, stood and spoke words that hushed the uproar of confusion and anger from diplomats who felt deceived. "I have sat quietly and listened as everyone spoke. But no one has asked why. If those carvings show a history between fae and warlocks then shouldn't we ask ourselves what they want? Strategically, they have surrounded Navarin. They haven't harmed anyone. What is in Navarin that they want?"

Her words sunk into the minds of the tribunal. Decisions were made and voted on to mount a strong offense to protect Navarin and Provence City. All interior entrances to Provence would be guarded day and night and the carvings would be studied and interpreted. The fae land, sea, and air defenses would be ready with lycan blood-dipped weapons to defend their realm. In Aradia, the elves would lower their defenses to study the warlocks. Messages passed telepathically between elves and plants. The elves had the advantage, since the warlocks knew nothing of them or their ability to communicate with plants, animals, and insects.

15

Once Hank was gone, Terra stepped out of the elevator. Still in Greenland, she needed her backpack. The cabin was several feet from her. She trekked back to the cabin through the snow, her feet cold and wet as she opened the door.

Bane leaned an arm against the stone mantle of the fireplace. "Nice of you to return," he said, as if she'd done it all on purpose.

"We were stuck," she snarled at him. M'ra might trust him, but she didn't. Her backpack lay against the wall under the bar where she'd left it. Ignoring his presence, she sat on the couch and stripped her wet socks off.

"Best way to get frostbite," he noted, dropping his arm from the mantle.

"What is your problem with me?"

He didn't respond, which ticked her off further. She yelled, frustrated with everything, especially him. "I didn't ask for any of this. I don't want any of it!" Clyde stood on his hind legs and stared at Bane.

Bane's face softened as he slowly moved towards her. "We don't always get to choose our fate, sometimes it chooses us."

She pulled her boots on and grabbed her backpack without checking inside. Bane didn't need to know the precious cargo it held. The weight felt right as she swung it onto her back. "Take me to M'ra, please."

He didn't respond in words but in gesture as he opened a portal. A smug smile on his sculptured vampire features. The teal light swallowed her, dropping her in the tower.

M'ra swiveled in a large suede-looking chair. The concern on her face said everything.

"I'm fine." She didn't trust Bane, but was gaining a respect and trust for M'ra and felt what she learned would help the realms. She didn't want any harm to come to a single soul. Most of all, M'ra and Rosette were the only others who knew what she was and would protect her from harm by staying silent. "A warlock tried to kidnap me, but he didn't harm me. He claims it was his kind who discovered and settled in the realms long ago but they were stolen from them. The fae locked his kind out."

M'ra folded her hands in her lap. "Tell me about this warlock."

Clyde jumped to Terra's lap then climbed to the back of the chair she sat in as if he too wanted to hear the story, even though he'd been witness to it. Terra described what she saw of his magic. His lightning whip and portal and his ability to see the elevators which she described to M'ra. She didn't tell her about the Stones of Hovrath. As much as she was beginning to trust her, something in M'ra's expression told her not to mention the Stones of Hovrath until she learned more about them. Instead, she turned the focus to M'ra. "You have lived many centuries and lived among old vampires. If I'm going to save the realms, don't you know anything that can help?"

M'ra lowered her eyes. "I can't help you." She lifted her gaze and continued. "That was long before my time. The veil to Lols has existed for so many centuries no one in my lifetime knew of its origin." She paused for a moment, her tone changing from sober to hopeful. "But there may be merit to what he says. As a realm walker you need to know that in Navarin there are carvings beneath the palace that tell a story, an ancient story. This isn't common knowledge and was only brought to the attention of the realms today at the tribunal."

Terra thought of Hank. Besides the physical attraction she had to him there was something about him she liked and possibly even trusted. The fae were deceptive creatures. "How do I find the truth?"

"There is one place you can go. As a realm walker, there are no borders there to stop you. The answers you seek, you may be able to find in the Otherworld."

Terra had heard the word before but wasn't sure from whom, only that it had something to do with death. "How do I get there?"

"Echo Valley in Thraves. It's below the mountain, in its underbelly. Only the shadow of death can let you pass. She'll determine if you are worthy. If she determines it, the gatekeepers will allow you passage. Listen to her, follow her directions closely."

The hour was late and M'ra insisted she eat and rest. Tomorrow, Bane would portal her to the border between Drakonia and Thraves.

The Regional Wizard and Warlock Council

Realm Walker

Latisha listened as Hiram and Winston relayed their progress. It caused her frustration but she also found it amusing, as these creatures had used their wits and magic to fend off wolves and vampires.

The wolves couldn't penetrate the capitol building so they besieged the city. As requested, they hadn't harmed anyone. Their forces mounted along the realm's borders didn't seem to matter as they reported only one way in and one way out. Where it led, she wasn't sure. What she was sure about was that the short creatures with tail feathers were crafty and probably mounting a defense. She hoped it might destroy at least some of the wolf army, leaving her with fewer to deal with.

She didn't hide her disappointment in the vampires. They'd been unsuccessful in sneaking into the palace as strong wards protected it. She'd expected that much, having learned the stories of the fae from the time she was a baby. Like the other realms, the fae escaped through a veil of sorts that even portalling vampires couldn't break through, their magic blocked by some unseen force. If all the stories she'd grown up with had merit, the fae were stealthy opponents who could attack from the land, sea, and air. They had only one weakness – iron. Iron, though, would not weaken the wards, it would only serve to kill the fae.

Hidden Passages

Her own warlocks in the wooded, colorful realm had their own problems. Everything there was alive and, even though they were hidden, were seen and trapped along the border by trees and plants. "We need to focus on what we know. Manning the borders between the realms doesn't deter them as it appears they can't go from one realm to the next. We also know the residents have entered a place we can't enter that is between the realms. I expected there would be inconsistencies from the stories passed from our ancestors. It has been many centuries. Vampires are immortal, could there be some that have lived so many centuries that they have memories of that time?"

Hiram cleared his throat. "It is possible, but I think it's wise to save that thinking as a last resort. Even immortal, we can be killed. If we combine our forces in the fae land we have a solid chance of taking the realm and capturing the King and Queen."

"I agree," Winston said, his tone not dismissive of his loathing for vampires, but Hiram was right. "We aren't doing any good in these other realms if they can't travel from one to the next. We post warriors outside the entrance to the hidden land they've all escaped to and we send soldiers to the fae land." He hid his disappointment in his operatives not being able to enter the land of vampires, but wasn't giving up on them yet.

Warlocks, unlike the wolves and vampires, didn't have sheer strength, speed, and increased senses. They had conniving and runes that allowed them to do things others, including the fae, couldn't but Latisha wasn't ready to show the fae that card. "We sit tight for now. They won't strike if we don't cause harm. Use your abilities to listen and gain intel."

Winston's face twisted into a scowl and he planted a fist into the table. "We have the advantage. We can take them!"

Latisha roared back, "No, you can't! If you cross the waters the water fae have poison in their scales that will kill you. From the air, other fae will swarm above your heads like mosquitoes and bombard you with sea water and other weapons. From the land, unicorns will blast you into oblivion and melt you into puddles. Do not attack!"

"Their weakness is iron. We are crafting iron weapons. In forty-eight hours we are going in," Winston threatened. It wasn't his wolves crafting the weapons but the trolls who lived in the land. They had smithing skills and plenty of iron. When the time was right, he would use the warlock to portal his wolf team to the vampire realm and the rest of them to the fae realm.

Hiram rolled his eyes. Wolves were a constant irritant. "I agree with Latisha. We listen. If we sit tight for now our threat becomes minimal and they'll feel freer to talk and let down the guards to their minds so we can reach in and learn." He would do everything in his power to keep the hot-headed wolves from destroying any chance of a truce between his vampires and the vampires of the other realm.

Winston's eyes glowed gold as he tempered his wolf. "Forty-eight hours!"

16

"Yu can leave that with me." Bane said, pointing to her backpack as the teal light from the portal vanished.

Terra cringed at the blood odor, strong from the falls. Its metallic scent toxic to human senses. "No, I'll take it with me." Inside were things too valuable to trust anyone else with, especially him. The Grimoire and pure soul were not up for grabs, nor was the book she found in Merla's cave. Once she'd left M'ra and was alone in a room for the night she verified all objects were still there. In his hands, she imagined he could do damage.

Passing under the falls was the worst part. If the smell wasn't bad enough, she'd be covered in blood. She winced, then remembered matter and energy. She called on the blood of the falls to stop falling long enough for her and Clyde to pass. To her surprise it did and, once they passed under the falls, started again.

She didn't have a map but she had the ability to see. It was one of the skills she'd developed. Her mind quickly formed a 3D image of the mountain. Stairs led downward, winding and pausing until they finally stopped. She wondered if that was where Tania went and met death. Were death and the shadow of death the same thing?

She used the flashlight on her phone to follow the steps round and round and down. It was eerie, even for Clyde who begged for her to hold him. He usually liked his freedom.

She thought of those in Provence. Her friends and Rosette. She'd been so disturbed about staying there and now was ready to go back. Why was the burden on her?

Duty can be heavy, but the weight will lift, the ethereal voice whispered from her backpack. What did that even mean? It never spoke when she wanted it to and offered cryptic messages when she didn't. She pondered the words until they reached the bottom. Glowing stalactites like the one Tania had shown her marked the entrance to a cavern.

"Hello," she called, her voice echoing off the walls as she stepped into the cavern. What exactly was she supposed to do? There was no shadow of death hanging around waiting for her. She was alone with Clyde in the damp, chilly cavern with glowing stalactites. They were beautiful, but the cavern was creepy. Chills rolled over her spine.

"Shadow of death. I call on you to let me pass to the Otherworld."

No response. Her voice echoed away, leaving her in silence. Cold shivers coursed through her body as she had second thoughts. Did she really need to know the secrets between the fae and warlocks? Did the weight of the realms have to balance on her shoulders?

"You can pass," said a voice cutting through the eerie silence and stopping Terra's shivers in their tracks. Terra spun around to face someone in black, long dark hair hanging from her wrinkled face. The shadow of death.

The arm of the cloak hung as she pointed a bony finger towards the other side of the cavern. "You must not ask questions or seek anyone. Listen to the voices: they will tell you everything."

Terra, one eye on the old lady, carefully stepped towards the wall. No doubts anymore this was who Tania had met when she came all this way after escaping Drakonia.

"You must leave that." The shadow of death's bony finger pointed towards Terra's backpack. "What's in there must never enter the Otherworld."

What did that mean? Was she referring to the glowing ball, the pure soul, or the grimoire? Terra knitted her brows. She didn't trust it in any other hands.

As if the shadow of death read her thoughts, she said, "Leave it. It will be safe."

If she was to enter the Otherworld she had no option but to leave it and trust the shadow of death would keep it safe. It wasn't like they were in a busy BART terminal. Terra dropped her backpack carefully. "What about him?" she asked about Clyde. If he couldn't go, neither was she.

The woman's old wrinkly face smiled as if hiding a secret. "He can go."

Terra nodded as she turned from the shadow of death and walked towards the wall which opened as she neared it. Two large harvesters with pickaxes in their hands stood outside a wrought iron gate. They didn't take more than a glance at her as the gate opened.

Darkness swallowed her as the flashlight on her phone stopped working. Shadows of gnarled trees covered the walls of the cave as she entered the Otherworld. She let out a deep breath to garner her strength and fend off the fear rising inside her.

REALM WALKER

Remembering the woman's words and M'ra's instructions, she stepped further into the dark world, listening. She imagined herself like Marya and Davi as they stayed on the path in the Aradian darklands. They were surrounded by danger but also protected by Matthia the entire time, unbeknown to them. She didn't have a Matthia here, but she had a Clyde.

As her eyes adjusted to the darkness, she saw more clearly the gnarled trees and a murky, cloudless sky. There were no signs of life. Shadows swirled around her then hid out of her sight. Murmurs came from everywhere. The energy of the cave felt like tense suspense music. The Otherworld felt like pick-up-your-legs-and-run horror music from a movie. Their words indefinable. She thought of the pure soul. It spoke to her the same way until she finally was able to make sense of it. She kept Clyde close to her chest. *We need to listen,* she thought to him.

She pushed everything out of her mind and searched the voices as she walked further in. The words making more sense, the voices more differentiated, until she heard what she was looking for.

She listened carefully, focusing her mind on one voice at a time, pushing the cacophony of others away. The fae saved the middle realms by locking out the humans who'd followed them through the frozen cave into the middle realms. That was a term she'd never heard. The middle realms, from what she understood, meant the seven realms. Humans existing in something called the outer realm. The X on Hank's chest. It blocked him from entering what? His kind had entered the realms. She hadn't mentioned it to M'ra. Why? Had she forgotten, or was it something else?

M'ra was 1,300 years old. When she was young centuries-old, even 1,300-year-old, vampires had to have existed. How was it possible she didn't know anything?

Her brain processing and still listening as the voices whispered their secrets. The humans were selfish and wanted everything. The warlocks were caught in the middle, losing the enter Stones of Hovrath in Navarin. They'd fallen into the lavender sea.

In The Origin, Marya and Davi entered Verboten from Navarin through a swirling disturbance in the sea. Bjorn talked about the disturbance. He called it a vortex — a place in the sea where the waters swirled. She put two and two together. The disturbance was caused by the enter Stones of Hovrath. That part of Hank's story was true, according to the whispers of the dead.

Not fully convinced she could trust Hank at least maybe they were on the same side; confusion, and the annoying need for answers. She needed to get there and find the darn stones, but had no idea what to look for other than a disturbance in the waters. If warlocks could enter the middle realms, presumably they all had Xs on their chests then he could enter too. *Be careful, the stones are very powerful,* a voice said, loud and clear in her ear as if standing beside her.

As a knee jerk reaction, she turned her head. A dark shadow, tall and thick, with glowing eyes, stood beside her. Her next instinct was to run, and she did, straight back the way she came, but couldn't find the exit. *Where were the gatekeepers, the cave that led her to the Otherworld?*

You can't escape, you're stuck, there is no way out… the voices whispered. She clutched Clyde to her chest. *There has to be a way out,* she thought. Clyde squirmed in her arms and she let him down, the leash to his harness wrapped tightly around her wrist. He stuck his nose in the air and sniffed then ran ahead, nearly pulling her along.

She didn't look at anything other than Clyde, focusing her attention on his little legs scurrying ahead. The gnarled trees popped out of nowhere as she jumped right and left to avoid them, keeping her eyes on Clyde who eventually led them to the gate.

She breathed easier as the gate opened and she and Clyde returned to the cavern with the glowing stalactites. A place so filled with the creep factor before entering the Otherworld now seemed timid after what she'd experienced. The shadow of death invisible to her as she'd probably shrunk into one of the dark corners. Terra's backpack where she left it, she knelt and unzipped it. She had to be sure everything she had in there was still there.

"Death knows no time limits. You haven't been gone and have returned in the instant you left," the shadow of death said. Her voice coming from everywhere.

She thought about the riddle. *Did that mean she was never gone?* She zipped her backpack. It was time to find Hank.

17

atter and energy. Matter and energy. She could control them, command them. With Lols on her mind, she pressed her palms against the air, feeling it move around her hands and tickle her fingers. Since the first time she was portalled, she felt she could see and feel the energy. Felt like she could part the matter, but didn't know how. In the elevator with Hank, she'd stopped it. That was her.

She concentrated as she moved her hands around her, molding the matter. "I'm a realm walker, I'm a realm walker," she whispered into the air. Accepting strength in her words she felt the matter part and pushed it outward then stepped through into a teal tunnel. Matter closed behind her and she watched the cave grow smaller until it disappeared.

Where are we? she thought. What was this place? Somewhere in the inbetween like when she stopped the elevator. Could she command it to take her to Hank or did she need his exact location? She thought of Hank but nothing happened.

Great! She did it again. *Calm down. If you got here, you can leave here.* The teal around her moved with her, growing longer with each step like she was stretching it. It wasn't a rainbow like the elevator. Pressing her hands into the teal, it parted enough for her to see trees with bright leaves — Aradia. No, that's not what she wanted. "Lols, take me to Lols."

When she parted it again she was staring at the same trees. What did she need to do? *Think, Terra.* Maybe it was the direction. She turned and parted the teal again. Dry desert air and sandy rocks — Drakonia. That confirmed direction had something to do with it.

The voice from the pure soul streamed into her head. *Relax. You command matter not the other way around.* That was helpful! Terra walked forward with a finger parting the matter. Energy bubbled around her finger. When it turned steady, like a heartbeat, she parted it. Each realm had its own energy and Lols always matched the patter of her own heart. Trees with colorful leaves and a farmhouse – Lols. She stepped out and watched the matter seal behind her. *Could she seal the veil the same way?*

Now she had to find Hank. *How had he found her?* He'd never said. He talked of myth, of fae and warlocks, of Marsidia and stones, but not how or why he'd found her and she hadn't asked. His looks and her defiance distracted her mind and sent her into the Otherworld and now she was ready to lead him to the Stones of Hovrath. Deliberating in her head whether it was wise or not, whether he was using her, she decided if the fate of the realms was on her shoulders, then she'd do it her way and it was in the best interests of everyone it seemed to find the stones and use them to barter.

Her distrust for him resurfacing as she chose to use sound waves the elfin way. She'd been versed enough, having elfin friends and playing elf had taken a plant communication class. Trees and grass surrounded her.

She pressed her hand against a large tree with bright, colorful leaves. Most trees in Lols, she learned, were sleeping but magic awoke them. Its branches wiggled or blew with the breeze. Unsure, she telepathically asked it: *Can you help me find Hank?* She pictured him in her mind and waited. She wasn't full elf, nor did she have any full elves with her to help, but kept picturing him and asking.

Finally, the tree wiggled, not just a breeze flopping a branch, but a definite purposeful wiggle, then another. *We can help.*

She nearly jumped out of her skin as the voice responded in her head. They did speak! *Thank you.*

Other trees' branches wiggled as if waking. It was the same thing Terra and her friends had seen in Lols the day they snuck out the curtain in the top floor of the academy and went into Lols. They'd awakened the trees who then helped them. They also helped them break into the baker's house where she found a crack in the veil that led to Navarin.

The one you seek is in Elora, Ontario. Be on your guard, he is not alone.

Thank you.

Elevators were everywhere and Tania said they were mostly concentrated around graveyards. *Is there a graveyard close?*

The tree didn't respond right away and she thought she'd lost the connection until its voice filtered into her head. *In town, follow the road west past the house.*

Keeping a distance from the house, she made it to the two-lane road. Potholes and a well-worn center marker showed its disrepair. Her mind focused on the elevators. Hank could see them, like her. He controlled matter and energy in the form of electricity which is probably what allowed them to see the elevators. Were they caused by the weakening veil? Did all warlocks see them?

A glance over her shoulder, and the farmhouse was barely visible. The road ahead desolate. *Why am I walking?* She didn't need to. Using her ability, she'd left the cavern and found her way to Lols. How hard could it be to get to the graveyard?

A hum vibrated against her ears. The familiar drone made her think of home as she'd fallen asleep to its sound. Not only one, but many. The bustle of the city called to her as she stuck out a thumb.

Stepping off the road, the car's motor changed as it slowed down and stopped. The car an older model, a classic with metal bumpers. An older man at the wheel, thin, gold and black-framed glasses over his eyes. A thin tangle of white hair on his head and a button up blue and white checkered shirt. He didn't appear menacing. After the Otherworld she didn't think anything else would.

She opened the door and leaned in. "Are you headed to town?"

"It's a long walk to town. I'll take you as far as my house."

She could take the ride or try to manipulate the matter. She slid onto the bench seat and closed the door, choosing the ride over relying on her abilities.

He didn't ask many questions as she stared out the window at the rush of color from the fall leaves. Maybe she should forget all about the realms and go home. Forget about the stones and the invasion of the realms. What made any of it her business?

The glowing sphere's words echoed in her head *'duty can be heavy, but the weight will lift'*. She couldn't stay in Lols. There was no way to ignore her destiny. Running wouldn't make it go away. It would only prolong the inevitable.

"That's a unique pet you have there."

The old man's words interrupted her thoughts. "He's a black-footed ferret." Clyde stood on her lap, his front paws against the window frame and his head watching out the window.

"What's his name?"

"Clyde."

"We're almost there. Town's just over the hill."

It wasn't much of a town. They rolled to a stop at a light. Buildings with large store fronts on either side of the road. Cars parked along the streets and an old theatre with a marquee. Large movie posters filled the windows.

He turned on the next road and pulled his car to a stop in front of an old home. Early 1900s style. "This is it. You be safe," he said, shifting the column gear into park.

"I will, thank you," Terra offered as she opened the door.

Back on the main street, she kept going, walking past store fronts with mannequins and colored drapes and window paint on a bakery that said warm biscuits and fresh bread. So far she hadn't passed a cemetery. People sat in chairs outside a coffee shop and she weaved through a group of pedestrians having a conversation with someone who literally stopped in the middle of the street.

She felt eyes on her but kept walking. Feeling like the stranger she was, she turned right and continued behind the building. She stepped away from the road and any watchers then poked the air, depressing a teal dot that melted away. Ripping her finger in a straight line she stepped into the inbetween. She controlled matter and energy, not the other way around, and commanded it to take her to the cemetery. A gravestone with fresh flowers was in front of her as she unzipped the matter. A smile creased her face. *I did it!*

Stepping out with pride at her accomplishment, she easily found the rainbow energy of the elevator. Its colors and warm energy swirling around her as she thought Elora, Ontario. She'd never been to Canada and shivered as the elevator disappeared around her, wishing she had the thick coat she'd worn in Greenland. Not once did she consider she didn't need the elevator but could use the inbetween to get from one place to the next.

Energy! Energy was warm. She thought about warmth surrounding her like a blanket and instantly the goosebumps from the cold went away and she felt comfortable if not a little too warm.

The realm walker thing wasn't half bad. It had advantages even if people wanted her dead. *What did the warlocks want with her?*

If only being a realm walker was like a magic ball and she could see where exactly he was. The town wasn't large, but large enough, and people didn't give her odd looks as they had in the Podunk town she just escaped. There were shops in old buildings lined up along the stone streets. The shop fronts were colorful and mostly brick with two floors. She wondered if owners rented the top half as apartments or if they used them for offices and storage.

Her mind was completely off topic as she took in the quaint little town. Whispers on the wind brought her back to her mission and directed her to a shop at the end of the street. A steakhouse and brewery. The energy emanating from it buzzing but not steady. It had highs and lows. She sighed; how would she get him alone?

She dug her finger nervously into the energy and matter beside her, drawing small circles. When she noted she'd punctured a hole in the matter she pressed it forward and watched small ripples move through it toward the steakhouse.

She wished she'd have thought before doing it, as surely it would alert more than just Hank. She wished she had some of the root Marya sucked on that made her invisible. The ripple spread out as it entered the steakhouse, dispersing at angles as it moved through the brick.

She ducked into an alley and hid behind a dumpster. It was all she saw to conceal herself. She pulled her shirt over her nose and breathed from her mouth to avoid the stench from the trash. Using her predator senses she listened for footfalls. "Terra, is that you?" asked the familiar voice she was waiting for.

She moved out from behind the dumpster. He stood alone in all his glorious beauty, his long braids pulled back. "We have to leave. Me and you, and I will tell you all I learned."

Pretend you trust him. Around him it really wasn't pretend. It was more difficult to not trust him as he had a hold on her she couldn't explain. Working to keep her cool and not melt into a puppy love puddle in front of him, she fought to keep her senses in check. It wasn't wise to play all her cards and show him what she could do, nor was she really sure how to recreate things she did, so she brought him to the closest elevator.

"You're not going to trap us again are you?" he asked as they neared the elevator.

"No!" She took offense. She hadn't trapped them on purpose. It was self-defense. "Take my hand," she requested.

He lowered his brows as if untrusting then let out a breath and placed his hand in hers. The energy between them buzzed. She wasn't at all sure where to take him, but brought him to the one place that came to mind where they could have complete privacy – Barra Head Island in Scotland. She'd done a research paper in geography on uninhabited islands in the seventh grade. This one was completely uninhabited, unlike some of the others that entertained visitors sometimes.

When the elevator vanished, the fresh sea air hit them. They were surrounded by the grassy slopes of the island that wasn't more than a gigantic rock.

Hank's braids fell over his shoulders as he turned his head, taking in the sights. "Where have you brought us?"

"Somewhere secluded. Do you want to know what I learned?" she said, surprising herself with how easily she was ready to tell him about her experience. *No! Let him speak. He has questions to answer.*

His dark eyes fell on her, his gaze and facial features expressing seriousness. "Yes, but I have to tell you something first. There are two Stones of Hovrath. The enter stones and the exit stones. Both have been lost, but it is the enter stones we need to return to Marsidia. We know the exit stones are here in the human realm. We know this because of you."

Terra stepped away from him. She shouldn't have trusted him. He hadn't been honest, and what did she have to do with the stones?

Reading her expression and body language he continued, "You triggered it. By the time we got to the storage room it was gone."

She thought of the college professor who was a hoarder of all things ancient and creepy. The entire storage unit was filled with stuff that gave her the heebic-jeebies. If she triggered it that's why they were after her. They thought she stole it. "You think I have it!"

He shook his head. "No, you wouldn't know how to conceal it. Its energy trail ends at the storage unit. There's more. Promise you'll hear me out."

What more could there possibly be? She felt like she'd been thrown into the midst of an ancient battle and was expected to bring everyone together. Terra fisted her hands as she thought of M'ra's words. She was a realm walker. A peacekeeper. It was her duty. "Fine."

Not convinced by her words, he proceeded cautiously, "I followed you with another warlock to an old house in Virginia. You went inside with others and vanished. A vampire, covered head to toe, killed the warlock with me. I got away." He stepped towards her. "The vampire wasn't of the human realm. It's part of our pact. We mark them so they can walk in the daylight. I went back to the house and found a room on the fourth floor that enters another realm. I haven't told anyone about it. I'm the only warlock that knows and I haven't returned but it's only a matter of time before they find it. They know there's a place between the realms where everyone has gone. You must warn someone."

His words sincere and his tone grave, she believed him even if she shouldn't. Each subspecies had their secrets, even the realm walkers. After so many centuries had passed she'd probably never learn the truth because it didn't exist anymore. "That's how you found me?"

"Sort of. You leave energy wherever you go. It's a trail but it seems… only I can see it," he said with hesitation.

She took another step back. "You followed me. You think I'm connected to these stones I've never heard of until now because I trail energy." Heat rose inside her with each word. "I'm the reason the realms are in trouble!"

He shook his head. "No. I didn't tell them about you. I… told the regional wizard about the realms because I didn't have a choice, but I didn't say anything about you."

If it wasn't bad enough that she had the vampire stalker, Bane, now she had a warlock stalker too. "You understand how disturbing that is?!"

"It's not what you think. I noticed your energy and wanted to learn more but I didn't tell anyone about you. I found you to talk to you myself. The warlocks don't know anything about you but I know you aren't like anyone else in any realm."

His pleading words didn't settle Terra's gut, but his soft eyes made her heart sink. *Why? Why him?* She couldn't stop the attraction she felt for him and the momentary pity when it was she who was being spied on. "What do you think I can do?"

He stepped towards her and reached his hands to catch hers, but she quickly thrust them behind her back. "Help me find the stones."

Clyde placed his soft head against her cheek and peered his brown eyes towards hers. *Great! Now they are both begging!* Clyde wasn't a begger. *You too?* she asked him, hoping he got the telepathic message. He didn't respond in words but wrapped his body around her neck.

She trusted Clyde. Maybe this was a turning point. A realm walker and a warlock tired of the lies and deception. She'd already made the decision to help him. His honesty gave her more reason, even though it upset her. "It's my turn. What you said is true, or at least part true, and I think I know where to find the Stones of Hovrath."

He laid a hand on her shoulder and she didn't jerk away. "I'm listening."

"There's a disturbance in the lavender seas of Navarin. I think that's where the stones are. That's what's causing the disturbance." It occurred to her that the magic in the stones might be cut from the same level 4 magic that created the realm walkers. It was the only magic strong enough to seal off realms from one another. She didn't mention that as she didn't want to play all her cards. She was a key to all the other realms and, on some level, Marsidia too, although it wasn't in the spell.

"How do we get to Navarin from here?"

Sure, she knew all the answers. "I don't know." She didn't hide the annoyance in her voice while her mind rethought the night in Aradia when she'd seen the realms split open with lightning. It told her more about warlock magic than Hank could. They had powers similar to hers. "You have magic, warlocks have entered my mother's home realm. I saw it split with my own eyes. We use your magic."

"I can't portal. I don't have a rune for it. When I found you in Greenland I used a gateway," he said, as if she should know that and, technically, she should but that wasn't her point exactly.

The downside of an uninhabited island was the absence of an elevator which meant she had no other choice but to at least show him some of her cards. If she went alone, she wouldn't know what she was searching for.

A teal blue flash appeared from the other side of the island catching both Terra and Hank's attention. A large half wolf/ half man moved through the portal, followed by others. Some with wolf heads and claws, others with four paws and human-ish bodies. Werewolves that couldn't fully shift or hadn't. She assumed they couldn't as no one would purposely be seen as partial human and wolf. They looked like the monsters they were.

Hank took Terra's hand. "We need to do something now."

18

There was only one thing Terra could do. She drew a vertical line in the air. The partial wolves moved closer, forming a semi-circle around them. Pushing a hand against Hank's back, she pushed him into the inbetween. He grumbled as he stumbled forward. Proud of her own strength, she didn't linger on it as the circle of wolf-like humans closed in. Once she joined him in the inbetween, she ran her hand along the seam to mend it.

"What is this?" Hank pressed his hands along the sides, leaving handprint depressions.

He had the power of plasma, why couldn't he portal? It circulated in her brain. "Are you sure you can't portal?"

His brows lowered in a sexy V giving her all the response she needed.

Instead of pressing the issue she answered his question, "This is how we escape." Thinking on her feet, Navarin wasn't safe to drop into but Terina, the lottery winning baker, had a ticket to Navarin in her house. Focusing her mind and energy, she metaphorically crossed her fingers and hoped they landed at Terina's.

She opened the seam and they dropped into Terina's living room. Terra's rush passage from Scotland to Terina's house lacked any precision as she and Hank literally fell three feet to the floor. Hank hit the floor first, padding her fall. Clyde crashed onto her and quickly slid off her back. The rise and drop of Hank's chest grabbed her attention. Terra lifted her head, seeing Hank's chin. She admired the strong jawbone and curve as she planted her palms on the floor and pushed upwards. He pushed up on his elbows, his face inches from hers.

Straddling him in an awkward moment, oblivious to anything other than her and Hank, she offered a goofy smile while inhaling in his masculine scent.

"Anytime," he murmured.

His hasty words cut her dream moment short as she pulled herself up and offered him a hand.

"You need to work on that. Whatever that was," he said, placing his hand in hers.

A female voice cut through their moment. "What are you... how...?" Terina muttered in a tangle of confusion. Her eyes wild, she drew back into the corner of the couch, but there was no more room.

Terra cringed, offering Terina a cheeky smile. "We're sorry for dropping in. We'll be going." She tapped Hank's arm as a hint as she walked away from the dark-haired, freckle-faced fae hybrid baker and towards the stairs. The yappy dog energy of Navarin calling her. Clyde bounded to the stairs as if he'd read her mind and waited on the first step.

The quiet volume of the TV drew Terra's eyes to it. A woman on the TV poured flour into a bowl then followed up with melted butter. Terra's attention refocused when Terina bolted from the couch. In sweats, a T-shirt, and fuzzy house shoes, she made a run for the door. Terra didn't care. All she needed was to get to her closet and through the veil, but Hank thought different and sent a lightning whip curling around Terina. It plastered her arms to her sides and closed her legs together.

"What are you doing?" Terra said in an aggravated voice. "Leave her."

In defense and confusion, he responded, "She was trying to get away."

Men! She didn't need a hero or prisoner. Were warlocks all this aggravating? If so, she reasoned it was their godlike glamour that helped them survive. "She's not our prisoner. We just need her closet!"

"I'm right here!" Terina shouted above the arguing teens and TV.

Their words hung midair as their eyes moved away from each other and focused on her.

"I don't know what you're doing in my living room, or how you got here, but this is my house. I shouldn't be the one leaving. You need to leave!"

Terra and Hank shared a glance and shrugged, then Hank's brows lowered. "Do you hear that?"

Her predator senses not on, Terra hadn't heard anything other than the confusion in the house. "What?"

His words deliberate, Hank stated, "They're here."

Tuning on her senses, Terra heard the pounding of paws, snapping branches, and heavy breathing. *Crap!* How had they found them so quickly? It wasn't possible. In disbelief, Terra met his gaze. "How? There's no way they could find us that fast!" She narrowed her eyes at him. "Unless they're tracking you!" She was ready to leave him behind and let the wolves have their fun.

"Impossible!"

Nothing was impossible where magic was concerned. "Last time was my fault, getting stuck in the elevator. This is yours." She pushed a finger into his solid chest.

He stared at the bands of bracelets on his arm. A glowing blue gem flashed on one of the metal bands, drawing Terra's eyes to it.

"Take it off!" she demanded. She wasn't wearing the comicay, not that she ever did, for this very reason. She didn't want to be tracked or spied on.

He pulled it off and dropped it onto the steps.

"Who is coming?" Terina said in a shaky voice, her chin high and eyes wide like a cat on a heavy dose of catnip.

They couldn't leave Terina, *could they?* No, they had to bring her along. The wolves were massive and looked more like full-grown bears, only with a dog body shape. Clyde chittered from the first step as if grumbling.

Terra looked at Terina then Hank. "She can't stay here. We have to take her." She continued towards the stairs. Hank followed, dragging a Terina like a scared cat.

Terina wiggled against the lightning whip. "No, let me go!"

Hank gave the cord a good yank and Terina stumbled and nearly fell into the first step, as she could barely walk with the cord around her ankles. It was more of a shuffle.

"You'll be wolf food. Is that how you want to go?"

That was a good one. Sarcastic and right up her alley. *Why was she relating with the warlock? Why was he so damn hot?!* A chuckle bubbled in Terra's throat as anxiety bounced in her guts. They didn't have time for Terina's antics.

The lightning cord vanishing, Hank tossed her over his shoulder as his long legs took the steps two at a time reaching the top of the steps before Terra and Clyde. Terra's eye couldn't help but notice the strength in his bulging arm muscles. Not that she expected Terina weighed much, but the ease of tossing the protesting fae hybrid over his shoulder was something Terra admired.

Terina protested and kicked her feet. "Let me go!"

The house hadn't changed from how Terra remembered it only a few weeks ago. She went directly to the closet, slid it open, then pushed everything aside, revealing the next door. Once she opened it, she ordered, "Go."

Hank lowered a brow. "What is that?"

"We don't have time to debate, just go!"

He stepped through with Terina. Terra following them. Once through, she ran her finger along the crack and sealed it so no one else could come through.

Hank put Terina down. She stumbled backwards until she hit the sparkly, fairy dusted wall. "Why did you do that? Now I can't get back!"

"If I didn't, the wolves would follow us in," Terra snapped. Between Hank and Terina this was more aggravation than adventure.

Hank rested along the wall of the cave, sparkly fairy dust dropping to the cave floor behind him. "It'll be dark soon and safer to get where we are going unless you have any more magic tricks up your sleeve."

Like what? Terra barely understood how she did the things she'd done, but he was right. If they waited until the cover of darkness, they'd have less chance of getting caught. It wouldn't be long, as the sun was low in the Navarin sky.

Maybe she could hide them in a shield like when M'ra had her gather the energy around them. If she could do that again without pushing the energy away, they'd have a protective barrier.

Terra opened her mind to the realm, allowing the image of it to form, its oceans and all its islands painting a picture in her mind. They weren't far from the disturbance, but the only mode of travel in the cave was a rowboat. It wouldn't draw attention but would take a while to get there.

In the seafoam green sand, Terra drew what she saw in her mind. Hank stood over her shoulder. They discussed the fastest route. Terra disagreed with Hank who was planning the fastest route. She'd been to Navarin and read Marya's journal. She was sure there was a current.

"Do either of you have a plan?" Terina said, hands on her hips. Her dark hair tied back in a short ponytail.

Hank and Terra shared glances. "We're working on that," Terra answered.

"You aren't doing it very well." Terina paused, "If I help you, will you get me home?"

Terra tilted her head in thought. It was Terina's boat. She was the one sneaking around Navarin, collecting fairy dust to spell her pastries. "Yes."

With a finger, Terina traced a path through a couple islands and the channel between the palace and Verboten. "If you follow the current you won't have to exert yourself rowing that little boat."

Studying Terina's face, Terra couldn't tell if there was a glimmer of recognition. There was something in her expression and tone, or maybe she was reading more into it than needed. She'd only met her the one time as a customer and doubted she was spectacular enough for Terina to really remember her.

When the sun set, the three and Clyde climbed into the small rowboat. The energy of the realm put Terra on edge as it bit and snipped constantly. No wonder fae were so snooty. She'd hoped to never return to the realm. Gathering the energy around them, she steadied it, hoping it would at least protect them from whatever was outside the cave.

Clyde sniffed at Terina's leg then pressed a paw on it. The fae hybrid touched his head. When he didn't jump away, she continued petting him. After a couple minutes he scampered to the floor of the boat and scurried under Terra's seat. His head poking out as he continued to study Terina.

Terina turned her head toward the open water. "The lavender seas. They are as my ancestors described."

"Yeah, nauseating aren't they?" Terra said.

Terina snapped. "No. They're beautiful. Look how they sparkle. It's like tiny stars in the water."

Terra didn't care. She wasn't fond of the realm. Its energy was already getting on her nerves. The cave seemed to be in a deserted part of Navarin as they moved away from the island. It had large trees with floppy leaves. Terra was reminded again of Marya's origin diary.

Terra couldn't hide them, but had the protective energy bubble surrounding the boat. It took some concentration as it was new to her. The place appeared deserted. She didn't see anyone and few lights dotted the islands as they moved past them.

The great island with the palace had thick trees at one end, protruding from the water. As the boat moved toward the palace, the trees cleared and were replaced with other trees with more distance between them than the ones with the floppy leaves. It was exactly as Marya described it. The palace was high on a hill over-looking the lavender seas. The shoreline sandy and open. This is where they celebrated the festival of dust and death. Halsey came to mind. She'd grown up in that palace and called it home. Except for a few lights it looked abandoned. Where had the fae taken Halsey and were her parents in the palace defending their land?

She chuckled. It was like some mega crazy fantasy book. For a second, she couldn't believe this was real life. Like she'd wake up and the past couple months would be a dream.

She remembered how Marya used the floppy leaves of the plant to cover her and Davi. She called on the leaves to do the same. It was preferred neither guard nor invader saw them.

A couple leaves fell into the water and floated towards them. "Grab the leaves. We'll use them for cover."

She and Hank reached for the leaves, pulling them over their heads. "What are you?" It wasn't the first time he'd hinted at that question.

She wasn't ready to tell him, nor did she want the fae hybrid to know. It was bad enough they'd brought her along. "I'm nothing."

"Not true. You sliced the air with your finger, making a portal, and tracked me to Canada... that was you."

She glared at him to shut his mouth and flashed a glance at Terina.

He got it then dropped it.

"I'd like to know too," Terina said, hands folded in her lap and an expectant expression on her face.

Terra closed her eyes to keep from screaming and sucked in a deep breath. It was safer for her that no one knew what she was. Sure, maybe she could find a way to save the realms with her command of magic, but what would happen after? No. It was better she didn't go around telling others. "The less you know the better." Cryptic, like everyone else. She was learning.

Terina grumbled, "I'm already involved, you might as well tell me."

The boat began drifting faster. It was being pulled as the energy of the disturbance became stronger. Terra's lips curled into a satisfying smile, saved from the inquisition. "We are here."

The boat moved quicker as it followed a circular path as the vortex drew them in. "What we are searching for will glow in various colors, follow the colors, not a color." A color, according to Marya, would take them to a specific realm. "Where they all come together, that's where it'll be."

Terra pushed the leaves off as she focused her eyes on the abyss. The swirling waters didn't appear to have an end.

Terina shifted nervously, her toes tapping against the floor of the boat, her eyes wild. "We're going into the sea?"

Duh? It wasn't like the hidden stones would be floating on the surface. "Yes."

"No!" Terina reached over the boat and grabbed a leaf from the edge and pushed it against her chest.

Terra hadn't thought maybe Terina couldn't swim. It was her boat and there was no life jacket. *Crap!* Clyde was an excellent swimmer. Terra was good enough and Hank hadn't shown any fear of water. "You can't swim?"

Terina shook her head and held the leaf tight to her chest as the little boat took a nosedive and plunged beneath the water.

Bubbles and sparkles of fairy dust surrounded Terra as she held her breath and searched for Terina. Unable to see anything at first, the water cleared. She didn't want a life on her hands. Finally, she spotted the edges of a large, floppy leaf. Ducking beneath it, she spotted Terina, holding it over her head. Swimming for her, she reached for her hand. The spinning current was strong and carried the leaf further down taking Terina with it, and Terra lost sight of her as she too spun into the vortex taking them deep into the sea.

Hank's form grabbed her attention as he pushed sand away from something. Water swirled around them, but in the center it was calm. Terina crashed into her back as the disturbance pushed them together.

Terra grabbed the leaf and pulled it closer. Thinking of Terina and her own lungs aching for air, she used magic to push the water aside, creating a pocket around them as she and Hank dug.

Taking a deep breath, she pushed sand away, revealing the top of a cross shaped at an angle embedded in the sea floor.

"That's it!" Hank said as he cleared the last of the sand away. The seafoam sand glowed in various colors.

To Terra and Hank's surprise. Their eyes fixed on the object, a hand reached in and grabbed it. Terra whipped her head in time to see Terina. A cocky smile on her face and a faraway glare as she clutched the object to her chest and took a step backwards in the wet sand of the safety bubble Terra created.

Hank lunged for her and sent a lightning cord toward the Stones of Hovrath. A smile played on Terina's lips as she pushed backwards into the water. Her legs disappeared as a shark-like tail took their place. The lightning cord sparked and sizzled around the inside of Terra's bubble.

Once the lightning vanished, Terina was gone. Heat rose into Terra's cheeks and sparks of fire exploded from her mouth as she screamed. *She hated fae!*

Hank's expression was one of defeat and surprise. "You're a fire-breather."

What? That was the last thing on her mind. She was. It wasn't her imagining fire stemming from her mouth. It really was fire. Satisfaction played on her lips then she remembered why she'd breathed fire. Terina was a hybrid water fae and, like her friend Cat, didn't change into a mermaid but a different sea creature. She let out a deep breath as defeat swallowed her and she lost her concentration. The air bubble disappeared, and water swallowed them and lifted them to the shore.

She pushed through the water, Clyde's legs and tail in front of her, and dropped onto the sand. A wet Clyde nuzzled her side.

"Now what?" Hank asked, lying on his back in the sand. He looked like he was making snow angels with his arms and legs spread, devastation filling his words.

She should have known. It was Terina's boat they used and she didn't have a life jacket. She could swim. Brushing the sand from her face, she sat up and noted they weren't alone.

Fae surrounded them with arrows poised and pointed at them.

19

Hank

They hadn't seen a single vampire until they stood on the shore. He assumed it was Terra's fire-breathing scream that brought them to their attention. Luckily, they landed on the island and not the shore where a collection of vampires waited. The warlocks had a pact and would most likely drag him and Terra to the Regional Wizard. Then he'd have to explain what they were doing and Terra's connection.

The flaky sand covered his toes with each step as he and Terra followed the fae toward the palace. Spears to their backs, they didn't have much choice. The fae in the lead stopped when they reached the palace and pressed his hand against the outside wall. A secret door opened. Hank stayed quiet and was surprised Terra did too. What he'd seen of her so far, she lacked patience.

Standing no taller than his chest, she was beautiful. Her eyes never stayed a single color and her small but shapely curves begged for his attention. He'd had a hard time keeping his eyes off her and had caught her undressing him a few times.

She was a bundle of something he couldn't define and the ferret stood by her side like a loyal dog as if they had some connection he wasn't privy too. Following the fae down a flight of winding steps, the air grew muskier and thicker with humid sea salt. Once they reached the bottom there were several chambers noted by the doors. *A dungeon?* In this day and age it seemed antiquated.

Growing up, his life had been filled with stories of the warlocks and the fae. Until he met Terra he'd never questioned them. Now he questioned everything. *What was Terra? What other subspecies lived in the realms?* A prisoner of the fae wasn't his first choice of activities. In fact, it was about the lowest on his list with the exception of losing the Stones of Hovrath that would take his people home to a hybrid fae. The only thing he felt he and Terra shared so far was their loathing for the fae and an intense attraction to each other.

The dreary dungeon was about what he expected; no windows, it stunk like mold mixed with sea water, and the one light that hung from the middle of the ceiling buzzed. Terra sat across the room. Her nose crinkled in anger. Hank sat across from her but not in the line of fire in case she spewed flames again. They weren't large, more like sparks, but next time they might be full-fledged flame thrower material and he didn't feel like getting burned.

Clyde sat next to her. She and the ferret were in lock step with each other. The ferret was a tiny animal, yet it stayed close as if protecting her. No… he thought again, more like guiding her. There was a connection between them that he couldn't ignore.

He drew circles in the sandy floor out of boredom and didn't take an eye off Terra. She hadn't spoken to him other than to chastise him and blame him for Terina. He was the warlock! His people needed the Stones of Hovrath, not her. It was their ticket home, but now he had second guesses and was far more interested in the secret of Terra. *Did he really want to go to Marsidia?*

He figured Terra's anger would wear off. It seemed it came in bursts, not that he knew her well, but her mind changed directions as often as models changed clothes for a show.

Her eyes fixed on the buzzing light, tiny little insects flitted around it. It wasn't surprising that bugs in any realm were attracted to light. Her expression changed as something seemed to click in her mind, her lips drew together in a line as if in deep concentration. He could only imagine what she was up to. Her command of magic was like nothing he'd ever seen or heard of. She unzipped air and matter.

A warlock needed runes to do anything, and there was a variety. Not all warlocks earned every rune. If she could unzip matter and take them into a gateway-type thing and make it go where she wanted then surely she could get them out of the dungeon if she chose. Right now she was broody.

The dim light shone on her short hair showed the roots were lighter than the rest. In the dimness, her roots were dirty blonde but outside, on the boat, they'd shown almost lavender, blending with the sea. He'd been admiring her since she stuck them in the gateway she called an elevator.

When she'd landed on him at Terina the hybrid fae's home it knocked his breath out, but her scent and the softness of her arm against his made it 100% worthwhile. Every minute between them she became more irresistible, as if a force stronger than a physical attraction was pulling them together.

Every touch of her skin sent tingles over his body.

Refocusing his attention. They needed to find the stones and she was the ticket. It hadn't escaped his attention that she'd stopped time when they were trapped in the elevator and had seemed completely oblivious to it. Either she didn't understand her powers or she was playing coy. It didn't seem her style to be coy.

An insect fluttered towards her, flitting around her head, then flew upward and escaped, disappearing through a crack in the stone. Against his own better judgment, he interrupted her thoughts. "Did you talk to the bug?"

She twisted her cute lips, her hazel eyes meeting his gaze. "I needed to get your message to someone."

He thought for a minute. So much had happened and now they were trapped until she decided to get them out. He'd forgotten the warning he'd given her about the warlocks' plan. In the meantime who knew what Terina was planning on doing with the stones. "I've seen you rip the air apart. If you—"

Terra cut him off. "You're the warlock. Use your lightning thing. It worked so well last time."

Her angry words slashed like a blade across his heart. He did trust her, for reasons he couldn't explain, but she had the power, not him. He was young and had limited runes and magical capabilities. She seemed to be able to do anything she pleased. He snapped back, "I'm not the enemy."

She wrinkled her nose and narrowed her eyes. "You tried strangling me. Why? Why were you after me?" As soon as the words left her mouth, she put a finger to her lips as if realizing something.

Really? She was going back to that. He'd been candid with her so much she called him a stalker. A warm wave entered his head followed by the words: *We shouldn't talk out loud. They're probably listening.* It was an immediate shock but once he put it together it made him smile. She'd figured out telepathic communication when she transferred a message to the insect and had figured out he was sensitive to sound. It was one of his runes. And she was probably right. He didn't see a camera or listening device but why wouldn't they have them in this ages-old dungeon? They had a light. which meant it had electricity.

He responded: *You're special. You disturb the energy and I pick up on that. I feel it every time you move through an elevator or the veil.*

Those runes. They look like old fae. They use it for spells, not in runes but spoken and written language.

His brows creased as a wave of anger forced its way up his spine. The fae stole their home and their language! He tempered his anger to stifle Terra from feeling it. No wonder his ancestors told such horrible stories. They stole everything from them, giving him more reason to get out. *These runes connect us to energy. Some warlocks have the power to portal and shift but...* His thoughts paused. This discussion could wait. Time was ticking as the fae hybrid had the warlock stones. Who knew what she would do with them? The only thing he knew right now was that she hadn't turned them over to the fae. *We need to get out of here.*

Her eyes widened and she let out a mangled sigh as if realizing a great many things all in a single moment. *I'm a realm walker, created by strong magic like the kind that created the Stones of Hovrath. I feel them as if they're part of me: that's how I can track Terina. There was a great war in the realms over a thousand years ago and my kind were created by the fae using powerful magic and blood sacrifice. The veils between the realms were created at the same time. Only realm walkers could go between the realms.*

Strong magic like the kind that locked warlocks out of the realms.

Yes, exactly.

If she was created with direct source magic and could go between the realms then maybe... his thoughts were correct and she could get them to Marsidia without the stones. *Can you get us into Marsidia?*

I don't think so. I can't feel it or see it.

But you feel the stones? He moved closer to her.

Legs stretched out in front of her, Clyde climbed onto her lap and rolled into a ball. *Yes, but I think that only means the great power that made them also made me. The spell anyways. It was the fae who created realm walkers using an ancient spell. I don't think it was theirs, but I think the warlocks...*

The door opened, interrupting their thought conversation. A fae entered, in a uniform similar to the fae who found them was wearing. It consisted of a dark green tunic and tight gold pants and boots. The difference was the ropes hanging from his arms. He had several thick ropes. Two other fae followed him with only single gold ropes and stood by the door as the one with all the ropes marched into the center of the dingy dungeon room.

He was notably older than the other fae by more than a few years. Folding his hands over his rounded middle he spoke in a deep, husky voice: "I'm Commander Wilcolm, head of the fae royal navy. I'd ask why a warlock and," he studied Terra, "a commoner are in Navarin, but I think better questions are how you stopped the disturbance and where is the artifact?"

So he knew. The fae knew what caused the disturbance in the waters. Of course they knew. Blood boiled and rose to Hank's throat, almost erupting in fiery words until Terra slid her hand over his. A trail of warmth moved up his arm.

Terra spoke. Her words believable. He guessed this wasn't the first time she'd lied to adults. "A fae hybrid kidnapped us and brought us here. She forced us to help her."

Commander Wilcolm lowered his bushy gray eyebrows. "Why don't I believe you?"

"It's true," she snapped. "I know the warlocks have invaded Navarin or somewhere and you probably don't believe us. I don't blame you. This looks bad, but we're kids, caught in the middle of something. We just want to get back..." She paused.

The commander placed his hands behind his back. "So this fae took the artifact?"

"Yes," Terra answered.

"Why?"

Terra laid it on thick and took the commander for a spin. "I don't know. We don't know. We're teenagers. It's not like anyone tells us anything important other than to be quiet and let the adults talk. You act like we aren't even in the room until an artifact is stolen and then you think we have all the answers." She raised her chin towards the commander. "We don't!" She said the whole statement in one breath.

Hank held in a chuckle as he'd never seen anyone do that. Among her magic was manipulation.

The commander stopped pacing and turned towards them, rubbing a fat thumb along his chin. "The seas are calm. That artifact is powerful and we need to retrieve it. You need to tell us everything you know."

"We have," Terra insisted.

The commander stood, his upper lip quivered as if trying to form words that didn't match his thoughts. "I don't believe you." He lifted his chin toward the soldiers at the door. "Escort them after me."

20

Hank

T he halls of the tunnels were dark, lit only by single bulbs in the ceiling spaced several feet apart. They reached steps that descended further into the depths of the palace, Hank and Terra exchanging questioning glances. Commander Wilcolm stopped when they reached a wall. With no farther to go, Hank studied it until he noted the thin lines no thicker than a strand of hair in the sand bricks.

The commander turned on his heel, like a soldier in formation, to face them. "Inside this room are paintings and carvings. Something tells me *you* can interpret them."

The *you* in his words directed at Hank as the commander's steely eyes met his.

Hank kept his mouth shut, lifting his chin high to emphasize he wasn't afraid of the fae nor would he help them, but he would read the designs and keep the information to himself. How dare the fae think a warlock would give them anything?

Waving a hand and whispering words that Hank heard and understood, the door jolted then slid with a rumble into the wall like a pocket door, only it was several inches of thick stone. The soldiers behind them pressed Hank and Terra's backs, ushering them into the room.

Like the last room, it had one light in the center of the stone ceiling and no windows. It was damp, smelling like the seawater outside and mustier than the last. The walls glistened as if wet and his nose turned at the moldy stench of the room.

"When I return, I expect answers," the commander snarled from the doorway as the heavy door slid back into place. Hank certainly wasn't helping anyone with such a nasty disposition even if he wasn't fae.

Colorful drawings dulled with age and carvings covered the musty walls. *Can you read it?* Terra asked into his mind.

He was born in the human realm and didn't learn of these strange realms until recently and was still perturbed that the fae stole their language. None of that was Terra's choice. *I don't know. They aren't a language, but ancient drawings.*

They stood side by side, Clyde hiding between Terra's legs, and studied the pictures. A man carried a staff with a curious golden oval stone. He'd seen it before but couldn't remember where. Clyde scampered to the other side of the room, capturing his and Terra's attention as the ferret lifted his front paws and stood on his back feet, his face against the wall.

Black burned into the stone in a pattern similar to an explosion. In the center was a circular blob surrounded by various levels of mottled darkness growing towards the dark edges as if singed. Terra joined him and Clyde scampered behind them like his job was done. What was it they needed to see?

The singed edges branched out into an array of lines jutting into a singular trunk. Terra brought her face closer to the lines and touched them. Leaves sprouted on the branches and buds grew when she touched it. Hank blinked, not believing what he was seeing. Terra dropped her hands to her side and jumped backwards in shock.

This wasn't drawn. It happened. That's Serenity Tree.

What was Serenity Tree? She was speaking in a foreign language to him. How could this not be paintings from fae ancestors? Why wouldn't the fae, habitants of the realm, not know what any of this signified? Terra once said the fae today aren't responsible for what their ancestors did. Hank grew up in a community where history was strong and stories were passed from parent to child. Had the fae lost track of their history? *Explain.*

The Serenity Tree is in Aradia. I've never seen it but elves claim it is… like the tree of life. Life comes from it, and without it life wouldn't exist.

Was she speaking crazy or was that what they were supposed to see, supposed to report to the fae? Putting the pictures together into a mural, there was an explosion from the circular blob and from it came life. He swallowed hard. Was the blob the source he'd heard so much about?

The source was the center of Marsidia and the birther of magic, but not a single warlock had ever described it. Warlocks are self-proclaimed guardians of the source.

What do you think this is? Terra interrupted his thoughts. She'd gone back to the image of an explosion and touched the wall, drawing her finger around the blob in the center. Dim spheres he hadn't previously noticed grew brighter with her fingers' touch. He counted seven as they moved toward the blob in the center until each collided, sending bits and pieces everywhere.

I don't know. I think that blob in the center is the source, but I don't know what the spheres are or what it's telling us.

She pressed a hand against her hip and turned toward him. *That's easy. These seven spheres collided with the blob. Stuff went everywhere and out of it grew the Serenity Tree.*

Faint voices and footfalls sounded from the other side of the thick door. The fae were back. Of course, they were watching and assumed they'd figured out what the paintings were about. Wouldn't they be disappointed. None of it made sense and they'd only brushed the surface. Hank gave the walls another once over before the fae appeared and he never saw the room again. None of them looked painted. They looked as though they were remnants left of an explosion from the collision of the spheres.

We need to get out of here. It was time. The fae were right outside the door and he was done with them, with this hideously purple realm, and ready to complete his real mission – finding the Stones of Hovrath.

Terra rolled her eyes upwards as if in thought. He couldn't tell if she was considering whether they should go or where to go to. She twisted her lips and lifted her eyes as if hearing something Hank couldn't. Rolling her hands together she opened them, energy crackling at her fingertips. When she let go it created a shield around them.

With a hand, she motioned for Hank to join her. Energy bubbled around him as they walked through the door and up the steps, past the fae. Not the commander or a single fae glanced their way or mouthed a word. If he hadn't been there he wouldn't have believed it. There were warlocks that could cloak themselves, but it was a rune. She didn't have any.

Like a never-ending mystery, she continued to amaze him. She'd gotten over her broodiness and they'd even learned something that might be helpful in the future. Moist sea air pushed against his skin as he took a deep breath. Like a breeze, Terra's voice entered his head: *It's time to get the stones.* She squeezed her hands together, her face scrunched in concentration, and a portal opened. Its teal light vibrated as it swallowed them.

21

The pure soul was full of surprises as it guided her to making them invisible and a portal that carried her and Hank away from Navarin. *How did it know?* It was a soul with a strong connection to magic. *Was it another realm walker? Was it Cyrus?* That would make sense. Or was making a portal the same for all subspecies that could portal? Her mind numbed with the possibilities.

Re-centering herself, the energy of the Stones of Hovrath pulsed inside her as if they were one, making them easy to track. The portal she created took them directly to them. If it wasn't for the pure soul she wouldn't have known how to follow their energy or how to make the portal.

Hank's expression said more than any words as he studied her. He was wondering what other tricks she had up her sleeve. None, she had none. It was the soul guiding her.

The portal she created brought them to the woods. The stones pulsed beneath their feet and she could see a cavern beneath them. "Do you feel that?" she asked, using words from her mouth instead of head talking. Now that they were away from the fae and in the middle of nowhere surrounded by tall trees she felt more at ease.

Hank's shoulders dropped, demonstrating he was at least partially relaxed. He bent his knee and pressed his hands to the ground. "No, but listen."

Sound was energy. She pressed her hand over Hank's to use him as a conduit to hear what he did. A wave vibrated from her fingertips through her arms and into her chest. It blasted into her heart, sending shrapnel outwards and causing her to fall backwards. She pressed her hand over her heart to make sure it was still beating. She felt alive, the leaves above her waved slightly with the breeze.

Scrambling to her knees, she noted Hank lifted upwards on his elbows, as he too had fallen backwards. His dark eyes huge saucers of disbelief. He didn't need to say anything as he lifted upwards and got back to his feet.

She let out a deep breath. There was only one explanation. Together, their command of magic was amplified. Sure, they'd touched each other before, but not while using magic. They were each a conduit for the other. If they used their abilities together, they were stronger.

"I felt that." He stumbled backwards in shock as he attempted to stand. "We are stronger together," he said in a strangled voice as he clutched his thigh. His face grimacing as he dropped to the ground, leaves crunching beneath him.

"Hank, Hank!" Terra repeated, terror filling her voice. He appeared to be in horrible, crippling pain. She felt helpless.

"A rune," he uttered between breaths.

She'd felt that pain, recognized it. It was the twin to what she felt each time a passport carved into her chest. Clyde had been her savior or rather his breath. Its warmth offered a blanket of protection from the extreme pain that felt something like she imagined getting branded caused. Clyde sniffed and stood on his back legs, front paws in the air as she snatched him and placed him close to Hank's clutched leg. "Let go," she ordered.

Between strangled short breaths Hank asked, "What?"

Frustrated he would even ask, Terra responded in a tight, forced tone, "Trust me."

Hank let go of his thigh, dropping his hand to the ground as he rolled backwards in agony. Clyde knew what to do. He stretched his front paws over Hank's leg and breathed against his thigh. In moments, the grimace on Hank's face vanished.

He ran a hand over Clyde's chocolate head. "How did you do that?" Clyde jumped over his leg and curled in a ball beside Hank.

"He just knows." Terra pulled her shirt down, revealing her passport.

Hank lifted a brow over his right eye in question as he studied them. "There're seven. What is the circle?"

"A realm. There's one for each realm that I can enter. I told you I'm a realm walker, which means I can go between them all," she said nonchalantly, like he should know.

His face lit up as he moved into a sitting position and pressed his arms over her shoulders. Excitement bubbling from within him. "Seven spheres, seven realms."

She could tell he felt quite proud of the connection he made and was a bit dismayed she hadn't thought of it sooner. "Maybe. We don't know that."

"Yes, we do. The seven spheres collided with the center blob." He pressed his hands over his temple and forehead. "Don't you get it? The blob is the source!"

Every cell in her body burst with a cycle of emotion, overwhelming her core. Unaware of her actions, compelled by an unseen force, she crawled forward and pressed her lips against Hank's. They were soft like silk as he snaked his arms around her and leaned backwards, pulling her with him until she was lying across his chest, lips locked and tongues exploring the other.

Her cheeks flushed as her mind dragged itself from the gutter and she pulled away, crawling off him. Completely embarrassed by her actions, she glanced away from him, staring at the patchwork of dead leaves on the ground. Whatever was between them was mutual. His arm sliding over her back, his tongue inside her mouth. He wanted it as much as she did.

What was she thinking? How had that happened? She'd completely lost control. "I'm sorry."

"No, I feel it too—" Leaves crunched as he moved closer to her.

Their moment evaporated and she cut him off. So much had happened. First, they were chased by werewolves, then tricked by Terina. The fae trapped them and brought them to an ancient, underground dungeon marred by the past. She didn't even know what day it was and, for the first time, glanced at her legs. Her jeans, now dry, bore the damage of the past however many hours, bits of dirt and fairy dust crusted into the seams. She swallowed, all she wanted was a hot shower, and clean clothes. "We need to get down there."

A finger touched her chin and drew upward. Hank's eyes studied hers. "We're connected. You shouldn't be embarrassed."

"I'm not," she lied. "I'm dirty and filled with fairy dust." She took a good look at him. Sun snuck through the bare trees shining over his head, catching the sparkly dust in his braids. His T-shirt wrinkled and stiff from getting wet then drying on his body. It looked like someone starched the folds as a cruel joke.

He laughed. "Me too, but we need to get the stones first."

She was beginning to think he wasn't so bad and they were on the same side. To confirm it she said, "One to five, five being the worst. What do you think of the fae?"

"Ten."

Her lips curled into a smile. They both looked like heck and shared a distaste for the fae. "Exactly my thoughts," she chuckled, feeling the energy of the stones beneath them. If they missed this opportunity there might not be another.

A stream of ideas on how to get below flowed from one end of her brain to the other. She could crawl through the layer of Earth but, without knowing what type of booby trap lay ahead or how far a drop it was, that wasn't the smartest idea. She could portal them like she did from the fae dungeon, but was Terina expecting that? That's sort of how they ended up with the Terina problem in the first place. She spliced matter wide open and they'd dropped into her living room. A warm tingle made her heart race, as she'd fallen on top of Hank.

Hank pushed his braids over his shoulder. "We should find the entrance."

Simple. His answer was so simple. Her brain trying to find a magic way to enter the cavern below when there was an easy human answer. Terina got there somehow. Turning her special vision back on, she traced the edges of the cavern until finding a lift door only a few feet from where they sat.

She brushed the leaves off the wooden door surrounded by earth on all sides. There was no handle. Hank felt around the edges and lifted it off. The hole only big enough for one person at a time. Several wooden steps led down. It wasn't deep, she could see the bottom as daylight spread through the opening.

Amused, Terra stepped away as Hank insisted on going first. Who was she to complain? Was it the testosterone inside him that made him want to be the hero and take the risks or was he readier than she to get a shower?

He may be a warlock but was more human or commoner than anything. In the realms, everyone was more or less equal. The females weren't the "weaker" species. In some cultures, like the fae, they were seen as leaders and more powerful than the male of the subspecies.

Once Hank reached the ground inside the cavern, she pushed her legs into the small opening and pressed her feet against the step. Clyde jumped onto her shoulder, wrapping his tail around her neck. She clutched the side rail and carefully felt for each step as she went down. It was like climbing backwards out of an attic. The strong connection she'd felt to the stones pounded inside her like a beacon.

As quickly as her feet hit the ground, the rhythmic call of the stones stopped and vanished, leaving her feeling empty inside. She grabbed his hands in a panic. "It stopped," she whispered.

His face grimaced into a panic that matched how she felt. Without words he walked into the tunnel ahead. It was long and dark. With Terra's special vision she saw it led to a large chamber. Terina wasn't more than a silhouette as she moved around.

The darkness of the tunnel grew brighter as they neared the chamber. Hank paused against the wall before entering. Clyde climbed off Terra's shoulder and slid down her body. His nose in the air, he sniffed then scurried behind Terra. Through Terra's vision she saw Terina, who stood with her back to them.

She wasn't the only one with magic, although Hank hadn't complained a bit that she was the one getting them out of pickles. He was the one with electricity that beamed from his hands. It was his turn. She pointed to her palm then pointed to him.

He nodded in understanding. A plasma beam coiling from the center of his palm. It wove through the musty air of the cavern towards Terina, looping around her middle, then bounced backwards, ricocheting on them, wrapping them in the warm beam. Before Terra understood what was happening, they were pulled forward to the center of the chamber. The plasma cord wrapped tightly around them. A look of satisfaction plastered on Terina's face.

From the corner of her eye, Terra noted Clyde peeking his head into the chamber. He'd managed not to get caught in her tracker beam invisible prison.

Laughter like that of Dracula filled the air, bouncing off the walls of the cavern,."You didn't think I wasn't expecting you?" Terina said, her hands cupped in front of her mouth as she blew then whispered the words 'blamaca fego feltsa margerum'. Through the thick dust Terra couldn't see anything until it settled in a circle around them and dragged them upwards in an invisible cage. The plasma cord and magic dust receded.

"I'm a warlock too. The Stones of Hovrath belong to no one. Nor will anyone ever use them again. Marsidia is now completely closed off to all other realms." She turned away from them, clasping her hands against the small of her back, and walked towards a blank, empty wall.

Inside the cavern wasn't much. A rickety wooden table that looked like a school Christmas gift a student made in wood shop and two chairs to match. A couple thick pillar candles glowed from the center of the table.

In a forceful voice that didn't sound like Hank, he said, "We need it to get back!" In the time they'd spent together - the day that seemed like infinity - he'd proved quite patient and… kind.

Terina tsk'd as she turned and wagged a finger. "There's no going back. It was a sacrifice your ancestors made. They lied to you, passing on that you were locked out and need to find your way back. It's all lies."

Hank's face drooped. "No, no it's not. You lie."

Did she? The voices in the Otherworld confirmed they'd been locked out, but not who locked them out. The magic used to create realm walkers and seal the realms was old magic and written in a version of old fae or warlock. The languages were close, related.

The fae stole them but did the fae lock them out? Was it a warlock spell that, like the Stones of Hovrath, was buried in the lavender sea for Merla to find, tweak, and create the realm walkers? It was in her backpack.

"You're fae and warlock?" Terra asked, interrupting the warlock/ fae argument ensuing between Hank and Terina. Their spiky words flowing like throwing knives.

Terina rolled her eyes and let out a deep sigh. "I guess you're the brains of the operation. Of course I'm fae and warlock!"

The fae was certainly coming out in her. Terra grabbed a strap of her backpack, pulled it off her shoulder and then unzipped it. At this point she didn't have much to lose so, without other options, she pulled out Merla's realm grimoire. "This connects us," she said, waving it in front of her face.

"What is that?" Terina asked, cocking her chin upwards. Candlelight bouncing against her features and the freckles beneath her eyes.

Hank folded his arms over his chest as if she'd been holding out on him. She had held out for good reason. He wasn't her best friend, Noah, who she shared everything with. He was a warlock who, in their first encounter, wrapped her with a plasma cord and pulled her into the elevator where they were trapped until Terra figured out how to make the elevator work again. No, she hadn't trusted him completely, only enough to learn a few things and get into trouble.

"A warlock spell used by the fae. I think it's a similar spell to the one that created the Stones of Hovrath." Terra unrolled it and held it up where Terina could read.

A grimace mangled Terina's pretty features as she read, finally covering her mouth and turning away.

Hank grabbed it out of Terra's hands and read then turned to the page underneath. His eyes grew large as he dropped the paper. It floated to the invisible floor of the invisible cage.

Terra read his god-like features, marred with anger and sadness. Their actions confirmed her morbid thoughts.

Hank spoke, his voice low and controlled, "Strong magic takes sacrifice, that spell used body parts and death to create magic strong enough to control the source from outside Marsidia."

Terra already figured that out. She was an ancestor of that creation. Questions circled her brain like a vulture around prey. *What exactly were the sacrifices? What was the source?* The sacrifices that made realm walkers she knew from Marya's journal. She didn't need to know old fae or warlock or to read the realm grimoire to know, but what was the sacrifice that created the Stones of Hovrath or the original veil between the middle realms and Lols?

Terina flattened her hands to her sides as she looked through the barrier of the invisible cage. Her gaze meeting Terra's then Hank's. "What your ancestors haven't told you is that warlocks are guardians and protect the source. The place where all magic comes from. That's why you can't have the Stones of Hovrath. Marsidia must be closed off so those seeking power can't control it, but one created with that spell can control the source." The words rolled off her tongue and floated through the air.

Their meaning didn't affect Terra at first. She thought of Merla's warning that if realm walkers were destroyed the realms would be destroyed too. She didn't mean the realm walkers wouldn't be there to mend the veils and play diplomat between the realms. She meant, literally, if realm walkers were destroyed the source would be destroyed. Terra gulped as she realized that was her. She was connected directly to the source.

22

"**W**here are the stones?!" Hank demanded. His words filled with fire. The invisible fairy dust cage rumbled beneath their feet.

Terina stepped away, towards the dirt-cut walls of the cavern. Like a scared rabbit, she cowered in the corner, similar to how she'd cowered in the corner of her couch.

Was Hank's anger dissolving the cage? They were stronger together. She wrapped Hank's hand in hers. It was warm and energy buzzed between them. Like in the snow with M'ra, she felt the energy building. As she had done then, she let go. The energy released like a shockwave, weakening the fairy dust spell. Sparkles blew outward, filling the air and coating the walls.

Slowly, Terra lowered Hank and herself to the ground, pushed her hand in front of her and squeezed, trapping Terina in a forcefield. No longer in control, Terina beat against the shield and Terra squeezed, tightening the shield around her.

A tear stumbled from the corner of Terina's eye. "My father, he risked his life to leave..." her breathing shaky, "... Marsidia, to protect the realm."

Terra didn't feel any pity for the warlock/fae but she didn't want to harm her either. It was anger inside her for being the abomination she was. It wasn't her fault, but the warlocks who created the spell and the fae who tweaked it. Merla. It was Merla. In that moment she understood. Merla did it as a last resort to protect the residents of the realms. When the realm walkers were cleansed, she was the only thing keeping the realms together. That innate magic she hadn't felt poured through her as she tightened her fist.

Terina stood like a pencil, her palms flattened against her sides. Realizing she was doing it made Terra no better than Cyrus, the realm walker who sparked the flames to destroy realm walkers. Her biological father. She wasn't him, nor would she ever be. She unfurled her hands and Terina slumped uneasily with the breathing room she'd given her.

Clyde scampered to a dark corner, chittering as he stood on his back legs. Hank walked towards the ferret and leaned down. His back to her, she couldn't tell what he was doing. Clyde bobbed up and down with excitement.

The candlelight bounced on the walls, illuminating the sparkles of fairy dust from the cage. She knelt next to him. Hidden in the shadows was a wooden box. He picked it up and carried it to the rickety table and lifted the lid. Inside was a cross-like metal artifact with stones of various colors embedded in it. That was it. The Stones of Hovrath.

"Don't. You will destroy all magic," Terina squeaked, tears streaming her cheeks. "My father hid the exit stones but never found the enter stones. You must protect them, conceal them. You must never use them." She slumped to the floor, holding her head in her hands.

Every ounce of Terra wanted to feel compassion, but she refused. The last time she did, Terina stole the stones. Terra dropped the lid to the box and grabbed it. Whatever it was lined with hid them. That's why she hadn't felt them once she reached the bottom of the steps. If anything Terina said was true, then she had to keep them hidden until she at least learned the truth.

"I'll take that," Hank said, reaching for the artifact.

"No." Terra pulled it away from his grasp. "I must keep them safe. I'm not a warlock or a fae. I have no part in your ancestral battle. I'm a realm walker created with a powerful spell that used the sacrifice of others. You read it. You know." Terra knew enough from Marya's journal to know what others had given up so she could exist. "The other scroll describes how the Stones of Hovrath were created, doesn't it?" She studied his face then turned her eyes to Terina. "The spells are almost the same."

Terina opened her mouth then shut it and turned her eyes to the dirt floor.

Terra sympathized as the warlocks stared at her. Hank's eyes narrowed as if he didn't trust her to keep the stones safe. Their relationship wasn't glowing and started out all wrong but hadn't she proven to be an ally? "I can't hurt you or the stones."

The Tribunal

Rosette wrung her hands as nerves crawled over her body like worms. All she'd done over the past couple days to help prepare the realms and stock the blood supply needed, and now none of it mattered as the special meeting was called over an entirely different issue that involved Terra. A commoner and warlock had been caught in Navarin and escaped through the thick walls of the palace. Only she knew what Terra was.

The fae, Allwyn, stood, studying his fellow tribunal members, his expression fierce. "The disturbance is gone. The artifact causing it, stolen. They claimed a fae commoner kidnapped them and forced their hand." If Rosette hadn't been so nervous she might have noted it wasn't what he said but what he didn't.

Ernessa, the testy vampire, guffawed, "They were only kids."

The fae didn't take the missing artifact so lightly, neither did the trolls.

Maglesh stood, his yellow plumage lying against his shoulder. "Yes, but what do they know of the artifact that has such great power? As long as recorded time it has caused the disturbance."

Terra, it had to be her. That was the only explanation, but she wasn't going to be the one to open that can of worms. If she started asking questions, they'd figure out exactly what Terra was. So far, they were in the dark and whatever was happening wasn't caused by her, although she was the only one who could stop it.

Rosette had to protect her. *What did Terra know?* Rosette needed to get a message to her. She'd sent her to M'ra, the only being alive who knew what it was to be a realm walker. She glanced at the vampires. The only one she dared trust was the young vampire Devan.

As if Rosette could read their minds, she understood they were all thinking the same thing. Destroying the realm walkers would be the end. Merla warned them, but they didn't listen. Her large hair weighing heavy on her head, she pushed the back up to relieve the strain, when something tickled her arm, pulling it back as a reaction she clasped a hand over the spot. A winged insect fluttered in front of her then buzzed close to her ear. *The warlocks know about the house. You must protect the curtain from Lols to Provence.*

Rosette swallowed hard. Terra. The message had come from Terra. She'd read Marya's journal, she knew Rosette was an ancestor to those of the darklands. A thorny, dark place surrounded by thick trees and an unbreachable canopy of leaves where the elvarin lived mostly in their insect form. It gave her and others who descended from the elvarin the ability to speak with insects and small animals.

Insects didn't have large brains. The message she'd sent had to be short and succinct. *Stay.* She'd figure out a message later. The fluttering insect landed on her shoulder, awaiting her command. "Do we have guards on the other side of the curtain in Lols?"

Hidden Passages

Her question raised a few brows, as several pairs of eyes stared at her. She hated being on display but needed to protect the residents. Lols was the only curtain anyone could slip through. It was carefully hidden on the fourth floor of Provence Academy but, if Terra's message was correct, the warlocks could breach it, endangering all lives in Provence.

She glanced at the insect from the corner of her eye and immediately began second guessing herself as silence pervaded the tribunal. Was the insect a plant, something to scare them into action? Were there warlocks already waiting on the other side of the curtain?

Lukas broke the silence: "We should have guards posted not only inside the academy but on the other side of the curtain. They found three realms, who's to say they don't know about the others or the curtain? They could be waiting, or could come through the curtain when their efforts fall through."

Side conversations and chatter erupted until Colton roared above the rest: "There are dragons more than ready to be at our service."

After little discussion, mostly Colton insisting, it was decided guarding the curtain from Lols was a worthy endeavor.

Rosette yawned from exhaustion. Each day that went by without hearing from Terra she worried. Was she still in Drakonia?

The insect sat squarely on her shoulder and she'd send a message as a back-up since they weren't reliable. Not just their tiny brains, but they had short life spans. The flying creature might drop off later tonight. No, she needed to speak with a vampire. There was only one whom she trusted – Devan. His sister Hyacinth was a friend of Terra's.

With all their houses filled with refugees, she couldn't risk anyone overhearing a conversation about Terra. The meeting dismissed and catching Devan on the way out was the only chance she had.

She used the time to think of a message to send and made small talk with other members as she waited for the young vampire to stop talking and head away from the crowd. Short and simple. *Contact me, tell me you're OK.* The insect's wings fluttered as it flew into the air and vanished through the trees.

Once Devan and the other vampire parted ways, she took the opportunity to catch up to him. "Can we talk privately?"

He turned his head, giving her his attention. "Sure," he said in a tone that relayed he was a bit unsure.

She glanced around to be sure they were out of earshot of predators with sensitive hearing. "Can you get a message to Drakonia?"

"I can, but why should I?"

Nerves traced her back and settled in her guts, twisting like a snake. She had to trust him. "I can't give you details, but my niece is there with the Minister. Please ask her to contact me."

Devan lowered his brows in a question he didn't ask. "I will do my best." His voice soft as if he understood. He was the vampire that saved his sister, Terra, and their friends when they went rogue in Lols.

23

After the ordeal with Terina, Terra didn't take any chances. She dropped the forcefield once they were safely away from her. It was impossible to go back to Provence right now with Hank. He couldn't go back to the warlocks and she couldn't take him to Drakonia. They needed showers, and clean clothes and food. All the fairy dust was making her itchy. The only place left was her home in San Francisco.

Warm water ran over her head as she rinsed the shampoo from her hair. Sparkly dust swirled down the drain. She'd allowed Hank to shower first as she hid the Stones of Hovrath in the hidden cupboard where her father hid Marya's journal from her. Until she had a better place, it would have to do.

She wiped the steam from the mirror and stared at her face, the image fuzzy from the humidity in the bathroom. Her roots had grown out, but not enough to trim the dark brown away unless she wanted a bowl cut, which she didn't. She preferred her bob. Shaking her head, water sprayed the walls as her straight hair settled each strand taking its usual resting place.

Pulling on a warm pair of sweats and a T-shirt, she collected her clothes and Hank's. He'd left them where she'd asked him to. He'd taken the time to fold them. Lifting them up, immediately his scent settled in her nose and she couldn't resist holding them closer to her face. Suddenly feeling odd about smelling his scent, she tossed her clothes on top of his and strolled downstairs.

He sat on the couch in the living room. His long legs hanging over the side as his feet were perched on the footrest. His eyes studied her, resting on her chest for a moment longer than needed. She hadn't put on a bra. She never slept in a bra and was conscious all of a sudden about her boobs. Did he see her nipples through her T-shirt? She glanced down awkwardly and felt relieved when the baggy shirt covered everything quite nicely, leaving everything to the imagination. It was the kiss. The silly kiss that came out of nowhere.

"I ordered a pizza and wings," he said. "I hope you like either."

She nodded, still feeling self-conscious even though she knew he couldn't see anything through her T-shirt. He was the first guy she'd kissed. She had little experience in the romance department except for Tania and a couple high school dates that never amounted to anything, but they were always female, although, she'd been attracted to males too. Her mind went in circles as she dropped their dirty clothes in the washer.

Closing the lid on the machine, she admitted to herself she'd been attracted to him since the moment she saw him, and not in the way she'd been attracted to others before. This was a deep-down urge almost, that begged to get close to him. The reason she'd gotten involved. Until now she hadn't admitted that part to herself. She could have walked away, never gone to the Otherworld or Navarin or found the stones. Now she had a godlike, gorgeous warlock she felt compelled to alone with in her home.

She pushed her hands over her legs and sucked in a deep breath before heading to the living room and joining him – alone. The curtains drawn closed, he hadn't opened them as she'd asked but since it was night why would he open them anyways? Nervously, she took a seat on her father's recliner instead of on the couch near Hank.

She rubbed her fingers over her nails, avoiding making eye contact as she asked, "What's your new rune?"

From the corner of her eye, she caught him pulling her father's baggy sweatpants down, displaying his thigh. She took a deep breath as her eyes wandered to the muscles in his abdomen. His private area barely covered.

He glanced away from his leg and toward her, a smile erupting on his sculpted face. "I'm not sure what it is but it has something to do with you. We're connected."

Headlights beamed from the road. An exit from the discomfort she was feeling. She jumped off the chair and rushed toward the door. "I think the pizza is here."

He devoured the wings, licking the sauce from his fingers in a way she couldn't help but watch as she kept her mouth stuffed with pizza to avoid talking.

He swallowed a gulp of soda and placed his glass on the table. "These clothes are a bit large. I'm grateful, don't get me wrong, but can you adjust them?"

What did he think she was? Her brow furrowed until she remembered what M'ra had taught her with the boots. She could shrink them. Letting out a groan she stood.

"Stand up. I'll need to… feel them." That sounded wrong, so wrong.

She touched the outside of his legs and imagined the sweatpants shrinking around him. Her eyes popped when she realized she'd shrunk them too much, showing far more beneath them than she wanted to see. No, she did want to see it, that's why she'd done it. Collecting her thoughts before he noticed the tight fit, she made them looser. "How's that?"

"Much better, thank you," Hank said as he sat and pulled a slice of pizza from the box.

He was like a never-ending eating machine. The slice folded in his hand, he paused before bringing it to his silky lips. "Did I do something wrong? You seem really nervous?"

She dropped the napkin she'd been crinkling in her hand. "No, it's been a long day. I think I'm going to bed."

"It's me, isn't it?"

What was he, a narcissist? No, she was a nervous wreck. The past day or so had been too busy for her to think and now, alone with him, her attraction was growing out of control. Of course he noticed. "It's not you. I—"

He dropped the slice onto his plate, his expression serious. "It's the kiss. I can't stop thinking about it either. I don't want to make a big deal about it but what I felt, I've never felt before. It was more than a kiss. In that moment we were drawn to each other like all the forces in the universe pushed us into it."

Like they were "fated" or something? She chuckled, causing him to crease his forehead in confusion. "Yes, it makes me uncomfortable. Being alone with you makes me uncomfortable, but it was just a stupid, silly kiss. That's it." She raised her hands to emphasize how unimportant it was, even though, inside, she felt exactly the way he did. "I've never kissed a guy. I know I'm bi, but I've always been more attracted to females. I don't know why I kissed you. Can we stop talking about it?"

"There's always a first time."

She narrowed her eyes at him. "Goodnight."

24

Holocall: Bane and M'ra

Bane read over the tasters' analysis twice before he contacted M'ra. This was something she needed to know ASAP. Now that Terra wasn't a mystery anymore and building a relationship, M'ra reassigned Bane. His new job was collecting vampire blood samples from Lols and what they showed was almost unbelievable.

"They all," M'ra stressed the word, "come from an ancestral line dating back to 56 A.D. and you're sure it's Delgon?" Bane's news was almost unbelievable. One leg crossed over the other, his hair slicked back like an oil spill happened on his head, she read his smug look. He was overly confident yet always faithful. It was no surprise to her that Terra didn't like him, however M'ra appreciated his talents and faithfulness.

"That's what the tasters confirmed."

M'ra couldn't fathom how it was possible a vampire would escape and why. Delgon was a powerful vampire. Did he experiment with humans to make his own line? Was it curiosity, or the nature of an ancient, powerful vampire? His death had been a mystery until his charred remains were found in Lols. "What have the intercepts reported about how these vampires are made?"

M'ra had sent spies she called intercepts to Lols to immerse themselves into the vampire clans and send back information. Each clan belonging to a regional house. The girl had been a wealth of information and was from the clan Idillia and the house of Hiram. The reason they walked in the daylight was a pact between warlocks and vampires. The warlocks spelled them with a mark that protected them from the deathly rays of the star. "Nothing yet. They are still building trust —"

Bane's words were interrupted by an urgent message from a vampire soldier. "They are here in Drakonia. Five Lols vampires seeking an agreement between their house and Drakonia."

M'ra's poker face didn't change but Bane's lips curled into a cryptic smile as thoughts circulated in his head. They sent spies to Lols yet the vampires had found them and wanted a piece of what they had. It didn't bother them that he'd killed two of their kind. Of course they cared. This was a trick.

"Where are they now?" M'ra asked.

"On their way to the holding rooms."

M'ra leaned back in her chair. "Perfect. Send me the girl." Her plan was to coach the child in what to say. She'd give Bane that duty. Last they saw the girl, she was dying of a lycan bite and now she was the picture of vampire health. She wanted to gauge their reaction. A truce or pact of sorts may benefit her vampires.

Drakonia was home to any vampire, but ones separated for so many centuries and made by a rogue vampire weren't Drakonian but commoners, with no connection to the realm. This subject had to be trod on lightly with glass slippers. If they could work something out it would need to include the spell that allowed vampires to walk in the daylight, then her kind would be unfettered.

Terra

She'd left Hank at her house. He couldn't go to Drakonia, but she needed to.

M'ra was the oldest being alive and the first realm walker. She had to know something, Terra hoped, metaphorically crossing her fingers.

She'd had an awesome meal of parmesan chicken with a salad. It wasn't as carb-loaded as she would have chosen, but good nonetheless and filled her belly.

She leaned her head over the backrest of the couch and stared at the ceiling while she waited. There was no popcorn but a smooth textured surface with thin lines. She perked up when a blue flash of light coalesced then vanished, leaving M'ra.

The veil covering M'ra's face lifted over her head. She didn't hide who she was in front of Terra. M'ra's walk was graceful, as one would expect from a leader, her shoulders squared and back straight. She was the picture of royalty – vampire royalty. Crossing her feet, legs closed, she sat on the chair across from Terra.

M'ra didn't mince words: "I hear you've been with a warlock."

It didn't surprise Terra that she knew. M'ra seemed to know everything, which is why she was here. "Yes." She wasn't here to talk about him and abruptly changed the subject. "What do you know about the disturbance in the lavender seas?"

M'ra folded her hands in her lap. "Nothing more than anyone else. It has been there for, well, since the beginning."

Not true, not true at all, but in M'ra's life it had always been there. Was she being coy, or did she really not know? "Not the beginning. There was a time when it didn't exist. An artifact created by warlocks was lost in the lavender seas and that's what caused the disturbance. It worked as a portal to other realms but the fae didn't know that. Marya did. She used it to get from Navarin to Verboten." Hearing the words flood from her mouth, her mind chuckled silently. The warlocks wanted the stones, their vampire allies invaded, and the whole time the Stones of Hovrath were right under their noses.

"I'm listening."

"The warlock I've been with is after the artifact. That's why the realms are being invaded. It's believed the artifact is a key to the warlock realm."

As was customary for M'ra, she read more into Terra's words than she actually said. "Where are the stones now?"

"Safe." She liked M'ra and trusted her, but was it wise to tell her where the stones were? No. At this point it seemed everyone wanted them; the fae, the warlocks, why not the most ancient being in all the realms? No. Only she knew where the stones were. Even Hank hadn't pressed her for their hiding place and if he tried looking while she was away she had a tight seal on the secret door.

Somehow apart from whatever was happening, Terra needed answers. "There's more. Warlocks come from somewhere called Marsidia and protect the source of all magic. Realm walkers are an embodiment of that source, created through a spell similar to the spell that created the artifact." And, possibly, the veil between Lols and the realms. She left that out. "The fae and warlocks share an ancient language."

"This warlock you've been with, he isn't safe in Lols. I want you to bring him here. I give you my word as the Minister of Drakonia that no harm will come to him from a single vampire." The pacing and clarity of M'ra's words showed a deep concern and curiosity.

She was right that he wasn't safe in Lols, not even at her house, and if they found him, she didn't know what they would do. Drakonia was a safe haven for her and she hoped it would be for him too. "Yes, I can do that."

Werewolves

Ryoni pushed the warlock's head down as she and the four other werewolves surveyed the vampire realm from behind tall, sandy rocks. It was a barren realm and carried the odor of blood. The strong, metallic scent forced her to wrinkle her nose in disgust. Vampires were the lowest form of being. Drinking the blood of others to exist and live for centuries, longer than anyone should.

Winston had grown bored with the simple, small creatures of the jeweled realm and their colorful tails and feathers. He wanted the destruction of vampires. A single bite from a wolf was all it took. She stayed low and moved forward, signaling the others to follow.

Ahead, the land was flat and tall buildings rose into the nauseating crimson sky. It answered her question about where all the vampires were. They were solitary creatures but lived in clans. They liked the idea of being close to other vampires but not working as a team, which is probably why vampires were so prevalent on Earth. The realm no doubt predated her home on Earth. All it took was a single vampire to make more.

The sound of a gentle flow of water tickled her ears as she sent Trevor into the open to check it out. In his human form, he closed the distance between her and the water in a few seconds. Even in human form, they had increased strength, agility, and speed. A werewolf should never be taken for granted.

Within moments, he returned, lowering himself behind the tall line of rocks where Ryoni and the others waited.

"Blood. The river flows with human blood."

Not surprising. She wouldn't have drunk water from here anyways and would have advised the others not to. A vampire was their immortal enemy. Ryoni turned to the warlock and pulled the gag from his mouth. "Can you make us invisible?"

The warlock sucked in a deep breath then gagged and dry heaved. "Untie my hands and I'll see what I can do," the warlock snarked.

She didn't like them either. They worked with vampires and hadn't ever helped the wolves with their spells. It was time. Ryoni closed the space between herself and the warlock and grabbed him around the neck. "Can you do it!" she seethed.

He shook his head, dislodging loose strands of hair from his mouth, seemingly unbothered by the threat. "I can't make you invisible, but I can camouflage you. You'll have to untie my hands."

That was the problem. Warlocks had powers in the runes they bore. To the average human they were ugly tattoos, but to a werewolf they were magic in a language they didn't understand. Warlocks didn't have many weaknesses. Ryoni's eyes glowed gold as she bared her wolf teeth, allowing a partial transition, and growled, "If you try anything we will rip you to shreds." It was a threat she'd fulfill herself if needed, enjoying every second.

The warlock narrowed his dark eyes. "I got you here, didn't I? I'm not on your side but I'm not stupid either."

25

Latisha

How did they lose Hank? Latisha tempered her rage by pressing her fingers against her throbbing temples. "Find him."

She'd assigned one of her best and, instead of dying like the others, she'd lost him. How exactly did one lose a warlock? He was possibly the one who bore the source rune and now he was lost! Rubbing her temples, she dismissed the warlock guard. Taking a deep breath, she released, feeling more in control until a knock on the door tensed every nerve in her body.

What was it now?! She waved a hand to the guards to open the door. As the Regional Wizard she didn't get a day off or a moment to herself. The responsibilities were great and not always rewarding.

One of her senior advisers, Ruben, walked to her throne, knelt and took her hand, placing a well-thought kiss on it. That wasn't customary, but he never addressed her without showing his respect.

Standing erect, he lowered his head. "I am the bearer of bad news." The musical tone of his accented voice tempered her rage at his words.

"What is it, Ruben?"

"The werewolves have forced the warlock you sent with them into portalling them into the vampire realm. A team of five. His message was short, but he thinks the others will be joining them soon in their relentless thirst for vampire death."

What a disaster this was turning out to be. She should have known better than to bring the werewolves in. With a sigh, she regretted having no choice. They would have found out anyways and raged when they weren't included. The warlock was alive because they needed him to perform the magic they couldn't. She needed to keep him safe. "The elf realm is a bust. We don't need them all there. Leave a small team and send the rest to the vampire realm, and any with a sun rune."

The sun rune gave warlocks the ability to shine a light equal to the sun for a matter of minutes. It wouldn't wipe out the vampire population but would certainly char any who came into contact with them. If they coordinated they could shine sunlight over a larger distance, covering more ground. The warlocks in the elf realm all had the cloak of invisibility rune that could be used for limited amounts of time on others.

She lacked any desire to harm the vampires in Drakonia, but wasn't taking any chances they wouldn't be hostile to their invasion as they collected the werewolves. The runes wouldn't harm any vampires from Lols as Hiram attempted to wrangle the werewolves. She was prepared to battle if that's what it took. All her forces carried silver swords to subdue any werewolves.

Drakonia

From a one-sided holocall, M'ra looked on at the five vampires from Lols. Two males and three females. Each appearing a bit uneasy in the holding room. She'd thought to keep them separate but it made more sense to see their reaction as a group. They wanted a truce of sorts. Maybe that could be worked out. It was her realm, but the realm was meant for all vampires. However, a truce wouldn't happen unless there was something in it for Drakonians – those she considered true vampires.

The door opened and the girl entered. She'd been saved from a lethal lycan bite, surely they'd know who she was.

The room lacked windows, as they were below the ground, but was furnished with the comforts of a home. Plush chairs and painted walls made it cozy enough. The girl carried a tray in her hands, laying it on the table she said, "You must be thirsty."

It was a good vintage of human blood, purified from any toxins. Contrary to what most thought, vampires didn't drink directly from the river. The blood went through a series of detoxifiers as it filtered through the rock into underground streams, from where it was collected. The blood before them went through an extra step.

One of the female vampires gave the girl a nod and flashed her eyes at the other four vampires, signaling them to drink. It was a sign of peace. She leaned forward and collected a glass goblet, bringing it to her lips for a sip. The other four followed her actions.

"I'm Rianna from clan Idillia, House of Hiram," the girl's words echoed through the silence of the room.

Recognition almost immediately broke loose on the vampires faces. A mixture of fear, curiosity, and shock. The female who appeared to be in charge held the goblet low in her lap. "How is it you are alive?"

Rianna took a seat in the only empty chair, a plush violet velvet one with stones embedded in the legs and arms like the others. "I was delirious. When I woke up, I was here. I don't know how they saved me, but they did, and they treat me well. I have my own room in the minister's tower and was given the opportunity to return. I chose to stay and become a vampire of Drakonia."

"Drakonia?" the blonde vampire in charge asked with a smug smile.

"Yes, that's what they call the realm."

A male vampire, his chiseled features carrying an expression of superiority and knowing. The girl had a similar reaction. Commoners had some silly notion that someone named Dracula was the father of vampires. It was only a character created by an author but, in some commoner circles, was considered to have legitimacy. Maybe there was something there. Delgon was older than the legend of Dracula but could have changed his name in Lols.

The blonde female vampire was well educated in the way of the vampires. She slowly drank the blood, savoring each sip as a vampire should. Surely, this was training Delgon taught his progeny. "Why have they sent a girl to talk with us?"

Rianna met the blonde vampire's stare. "Everyone here has a job and we don't question the job the minister assigns. It is a sign of privilege to get orders directly from her."

Impressed with the girl and Bane's coaching abilities, M'ra was growing to like the girl more each day.

A red-headed female vampire spoke, her words displaying her impatience, "When do we speak with the minister?"

"You don't," Rianna's words concise. "She will entertain a meeting with Hiram, but only if you answer her questions honestly and submit to a blood test."

The blonde vampire shot a disdainful glance at the red-head. "Of course we will."

Another call blinked from the comicay on M'ra's wrist. She depressed the center and lowered the volume on the one-way holocall.

The low male voice, from one of her most trusted, sent a ripple of displeasure coursing down her spine. *We have a wolf problem. They are camouflaged from our sight, but not our noses. Their scent is heading toward the city.*

Wolves needed help to enter Drakonia and commoner wolves couldn't enter through the curtain without a Drakonian passport. *Stay hidden and follow them. Let's see what they're after. And be careful.*

26

The house was empty when Terra returned. Her first thought was that Hank had found the stones and left. Panic clutched her gut until she remembered she could see what others couldn't. Opening her realm walker sight, she got a complete visual of the house which included the secret compartment where she hid the Stones. The artifact was still there. With Hank gone, it was time to find a better hiding place.

She lowered her backpack and dropped it onto the couch. Everything in her backpack needed a safe spot. Clyde bounced onto the couch then leaned over the side and pressed his chocolate paws onto the top of her backpack. "What is it?" she asked, as if the ferret would answer in words.

He rubbed his nose along the zipper. "I should unzip it?" she asked. He didn't answer in sound but turned his head toward her.

"OK." Once she unzipped the backpack she collected the box that held the pure soul. He'd been obsessed with it since he found it. All she knew of it was that it had a strong magic connection when it was alive and it spoke to her. It knew things only a realm walker would. She teased the idea that it was Cyrus, her biological father, but that didn't add up. Its disembodied voice was female.

She lifted the lid on the box and Clyde peeked his head over the side. "Where do I hide you?" she whispered.

Not expecting a response, she jumped when it answered. "You are a realm walker, own it." The voice sounded almost irritated.

Own it. What on Earth did that even mean? How did she own what she was? There was no one to teach her. Meesha, her lycan friend, was awesome as an instructor but couldn't teach her to be a realm walker. It wasn't innate.

"Yes it is," the voice responded.

She hadn't spoken the words. Now the soul was in her head? "Then why did you have to show me how to portal, how to climb through rock, how to—"

The voice cut her off. "Open your mind and control it. Never let it control you."

Control it, echoed against her skull. The spell created veils between realms and curtains that required a passport for that realm to move through them. M'ra said Cyrus made Provence bigger. Provence City itself was a creation made from the same spell as realm walkers with its nauseating myrrh-eucalyptus air, temperature control, and fake sky. It had been created that way by realm walkers. The idea of having that much power made every hair on her head stand at attention. She didn't want it.

Maybe none of the first realm walkers or their ancestors wanted it, but they weren't all into it like her. It wasn't a choice. That's why the voice warned her not to let it control her. Power, that's what people wanted. She wanted none of it. Sitting in her childhood home, phantom images of her and her father living their lives flashed in front of her eyes. He knew what she was and gave her a normal childhood. She was grateful for that, but it was over.

After careful thought, she understood the message from the pure soul. She could do anything, but what she did had to be done to help others, not herself. If she became selfish the power would go to her head. She'd become her biological father.

When she cut matter and entered the inbetween place it was teal and warm. It had no decoration or furniture. It was a place that could be molded. Her eyes enlarged. That was it!

Carefully, she placed the pure soul in her backpack and collected the Stones from the secret compartment then ran a finger in front of her and stepped into the inbetween. This was a place she could learn and play, molding matter as she saw fit. She envisioned a bright sun above her, its warmth radiating on her head and shoulders. For shade, she pictured a tree. Its trunk wide, with flexible branches that cascaded from the top, draping over her like an umbrella. The leaves small with petite, colorful buds. Beneath her feet tall, green-bluish-silver grass like the leaves on some of the trees in Provence.

The grass spread as far as the eye could see and over a small hill. She walked up the hill and stared to the field below, imagining California Golden poppies. The delicate orange flowers rose from the ground and within moments the entire field was a brilliant display of the golden flowers.

In disbelief of what she created, she pressed a foot into the grass and watched the sprigs bounce back then leaned down and touched them. Each blade was soft on her fingers. Running a hand over the tops, she smiled.

She ran a hand over the bark of the tree she created. Its bark rough. Her mind carved a hole in the bottom of the wide trunk. Inside it, she placed the box containing the pure soul, next to that the wooden box with the Stones of Hovrath and, on top, Merla's scroll and the book Halsey used to find the scroll. Satisfied, she waved a hand in front of the hole in the trunk, sealing it. As the only realm walker, no one else could enter her special place in the inbetween. Everything hidden in the trunk would be safe.

There was one thing missing. Her sanctuary needed wind. If she could control energy, then she could make a breeze. Not a strong wind, but one that could blow the dangling branches of the tree without knocking the blooms off. Now she was satisfied.

The silence of the house hit her hard as she returned to her father's office. A buzzing caught her ear and she twisted her head to face a small flying insect. Its iridescent wings and rounded body not of Lols. It was the bug she spoke to when she and Hank were trapped in Navarin in the musky, gross dungeon. She held out her hand and it landed on her palm. *Did you give Rosette the message? Contact her. Tell her you're OK.*

A smile creased Terra's face. It worked. With the insect in her palm, she drifted up the stairs and to the small balcony. Opening the French doors, she stepped into the chilly autumn air. *Thank you. Fly home.*

The insect's colorful wings fluttered as it lifted from her palm, disappearing into the blue sky. She hadn't known that trick would work. How could insects go through veils when larger beings couldn't? Were the veils specific about the size of who could come and go, or specific to types of organisms like the curtains?

Shutting the doors, she thought. Rosette cared enough to want to know how she was. The stuffy elf had come a long way from *Lady Betty* to someone who cared for Terra.

Her thoughts rolled to her friends. She wondered how they were doing. They had to be curious about her since they hadn't seen her in days. She wasn't sure at this point how many days she'd been gone. If she could create all that she did, surely she could return to Provence and spy without anyone noticing, maybe even visit Rosette.

Opening the fabric of matter, she entered the inbetween. The breeze she made blew her short hair over her ears. She pushed the strands behind them and thought of Provence City. That wasn't enough. She couldn't go as herself, not after being missing.

Rummaging through her room she put on a hat then laughed at herself. If she could make her own space, surely she could remake herself, but who or what did she want to be?

Trying out a few different looks, she finally decided on an elf, after all her mother was the realm walker of Aradia. Provence buzzed with commotion from all the immigrants seeking asylum and she'd fit right in. She'd left Clyde home, as surely he'd draw attention to her and she wanted to be invisible. She weaved her way through the crowds, seeking a familiar face.

There were just too many people milling about to find anyone, until a tall figure appeared above the heads of others. The twists in her hair familiar, Terra pushed through the crowd until she was walking beside Meesha, her good friend and magic tutor. As a lycan she was tall and toned. "Meesha."

Meesha paused and cocked her head down and to the side, studying Terra's face. After a moment, recollection registered in Meesha's dark eyes. "Terra?"

"Yeah, where is everyone?"

Meesha looped an arm around Terra's and pulled her away from the crowd and towards the woods surrounding the city. "Where have you been?" she asked, concern mottling her sculpted features.

That was a super loaded question. She'd been all over. It started with her escape from Provence. They continued walking into the woods as Terra relayed the story, keeping her voice low as she didn't need a predator species overhearing them.

Meesha parked under a silver-leafed tree and turned on her heel, facing Terra. "That was you in Navarin." She paused. "I saw Halsey yesterday. She told me someone matching your description was captured in Navarin along with a warlock."

It was a good thing she thought to disguise herself. "Who else knows?"

"Kinzo, Kayln, Hyacinth, Caspen, Nalysse. Halsey called us all together. She thought we'd want to know, we've all been worried. You vanished on us."

"Yeah, about that. I'm ummm…" She pushed onto her tiptoes and motioned for Meesha to lower her ear. "I'm a realm walker."

Meesha lifted her head after hearing the words and mushed her eyebrows. "What is that?"

"Call everyone together and I'll tell you all."

It took the group a half an hour or so to drop what they were doing and join Terra and Meesha. She was met with hugs as well as scoldings for not saying anything to them. Halsey responded that she couldn't sneak away at the moment. Terra felt bad for her. As a diama she could imagine how closely they were guarding her and how horrible it would be to lose freedom. It was the first time she'd ever really thought of Halsey compassionately.

Collecting her thoughts, she couldn't talk to them in Provence. It was too dangerous. Squeals and heated discussion would be sure to follow. Her words could be in earshot of anyone and she didn't need it getting around that a realm walker existed. Her kind was hated. They were cleansed from existence, except for her as her mother had swept her into Lols before her birth.

"I'm sorry. There's so much to tell but I can't do it here. Do as I ask and don't speak. What I'm about to do will shock all of you." She pushed her finger into the fabric of the realm and pulled it open, revealing her sanctuary.

Gasps followed her actions and six sets of eyes stared at her, all with a question mark in them. "Go, now."

Her words urgent, each stepped into her sanctuary and the mumbles and questions started. 'What is this?' 'How?' 'Where are we?' 'What are you?' 'Where are we?'

She silenced them. "I'm something called a realm walker. You can't ever mutter that word. My kind was created centuries ago during a great war to bring peace and they did, but eventually it was learned they had great command of magic and they were cleansed from existence."

"'Cleansed', you mean," Kayln said, drawing an invisible RIP across her throat with her finger.

Terra nodded. "I'm the only one. My parents took me to Lols but my mom returned here and was… cleansed."

"I'm so sorry." Hyacinth wrapped an arm around her shoulder. Terra appreciated her friend's comforting embrace.

Kinzo narrowed an eye. "What do realm walkers do?"

A broad smile erupted across Terra's face. "This." She held her hands out. "I created this place. It's my place and no one can come here without me. A strong fae spell created realm walkers, along with the veils and curtains. All the realms had been open, anyone could travel to and from a realm until the spell."

"Level 4 magic. It uses sacrifice." Kayln swallowed like a lump was stuck in her throat.

The sobering reality Terra hadn't agreed with. It wasn't right that others had to die so she could live, but it was what it was and she couldn't change the past.

Caspen nudged Hyacinth in their secret lovers' language. "If you were created to bring peace and can make all this," her eyes rolled across the silver grassy field, "then the sacrifice created beauty, something good from the bad… the warlocks, wolves, and vampires have pulled out of the realms and… entered Drakonia."

They didn't have passports. How could they cross the veil? Certainly, they didn't go through the curtain. It took Terra a moment to process and a lump formed in her stomach. M'ra. "I have to go. Rosette. Please tell her I'm fine." She opened the realm to Provence and watched as her friends left her. Zipping it back together she returned to her house and stepped out into her bedroom.

"Where have you been?" Hank's deep voice asked from the doorway. He stood under the frame, his hands pushed out against it.

Her? Where has she been? Where had he *been?* There wasn't time. She needed to get to Drakonia. But why had everyone gone there? The artifact had been in Navarin. There was nothing in Drakonia but desert, a blood river, sand, and a crimson sky. "Why would warlocks go to Drakonia?"

He dropped his hands to his sides, his beautiful face twisting in confusion. "They wouldn't."

"They have - and the wolves and vampires!" Her voice raised several octaves as she spat the words out.

He shook his head. "Wolves hate vampires, vampires hate wolves and warlocks—" his words cut off mid-thought.

"Spit it out!"

"It's a human battle of the ages and it is falling into these realms. They aren't there for Drakonia. The wolves are blood-thirsty for vampires and probably there to destroy them. An entire realm of vampires. It's the only thing. The vampires are there to fight alongside the Drakonian vampires. Warlocks will destroy it all. They will fight for themselves." His words solemn.

Terra opened a portal around them. There wasn't a second to waste.

27

The warm light sizzled as the portal closed. Terra's eyes widened as she ducked to avoid a wolf, its brown underbelly moving over her head as it leaped at a vampire. Rolling out of the way, careful not to put force on her backpack where Clyde was safely tucked, she bumped into the legs of another vampire. She'd dropped them in the middle of the battle between vampires and wolves. She really needed to work on her portalling skills. A hand grabbed her arm and pulled her onto her feet.

A growling wolf ran at her and Hank. She stumbled as he pulled her along, dodging claws, teeth, and swords slicing through the air. Not glancing over her shoulder, she kept her eyes focused on the lowlands until they were climbing the sandy rocks.

Hank let go of her hand and they scrambled up the rocks together and stood on a small rocky knoll, staring at the bloody battle beneath them. Wolves in their form charging vampires who escaped with their speed and portal abilities. An orange cat that looked much like a tiger snarled at a wolf as they circled each other, both baring their sharp teeth. Swords made from silver plunged into the heads and bellies of wolves. She had to do something.

Hank put an arm around her. "We can't watch the massacre. We need to do something."

We, it wasn't just her but we. He was right. Together they were stronger, but how would they get the attention of all the vampires and wolves in the valley? She could breathe fire, but could she make enough to flash flames over their heads? Hank was sensitive to sound, could they use sound energy at a high pitch to cripple them? Predators had extremely acute hearing, surely it could work.

Terra opened her mouth to speak when a teal light flashed across the valley from them on a cliff, behind it blood streamed from the falls. Using her predator vision she gasped as the teal light vanished and M'ra stood alone on the cliff. Swords stopped clinking, growling dropped off, as eyes lifted upwards. Terra swallowed hard and, without thinking, created a portal.

The light dissipated, leaving them on the cliff beside M'ra. All Terra thought of was the danger M'ra was in. She was the minister of the realm and needed to be protected at all costs. Vampire soldiers could fight on the ground and take care of the wolves, but she couldn't be placed in harm's way. Terra swallowed hard, a lump in the back of her throat. "What are you doing?"

M'ra placed her hands on Terra's shoulders. "You are a realm walker like I was. What you say I think is true. In my day we didn't understand all of our power. It was Cyrus who showed what realm walkers are capable of. If you are the source, then you can do anything."

That word came up again. The source. What was it? *A globby ball thing,* she answered her own question, thinking back to the carvings and pictures in the fae lower dungeon. If what they saw was what Hank thought it was then the blobby thing was the source. "I don't understand."

"I do. The source is where magic comes from. Everything you see, all the realms and life came from it," Hank stated. He stepped in front of M'ra, his back to the battle below. "It's true. It's all true..."

M'ra nodded. "Every word. You must keep her safe, protect her as you are sworn to guard the source."

Terra couldn't believe her ears. M'ra knew more than she'd let on. M'ra glanced down at Clyde. "And him. He was sent to you."

Hank drew his eyebrows together. "I don't understand."

M'ra knitted her brows. "You are a guardian of the source and must protect her. If anything happens to her, before she can birth another, all this will end. The source will die with her."

Terra didn't understand the nonsense. She understood werewolves and vampires were viciously attacking each other and M'ra was at risk. "We need to get you out of here. It's not safe."

"No! This is my realm. I've hidden myself too long. Every realm walker feels a steady rhythm inside them like a second heartbeat. I haven't felt it in years until today. For a moment it returned and showed me you and him and the future." She turned her eyes to Hank. "It spoke to me in feelings. You and Terra are connected. You must learn to utilize the source together. There are things worse than what you see below us."

Terra felt the pulse in her when she created her sanctuary in the inbetween and, before that, possibly all of her life. She'd avoided it, wanting the normal life her father gave her. Even now she didn't want the power. She wanted to go home to San Francisco and finish her senior year then go to college like her friends. None of that was remotely possible now. She couldn't return, not after all she'd been through and the message the steady beat within her sent. The message she'd always avoided.

M'ra wrapped her hand around Terra and the other around Hank, pulling them together. "You are stronger together. The source speaks to both of you. Warlocks are guardians of the source and he is guardian of you. The battle ahead will need both of you to defeat it."

The warmth of Hank's grasp pushed energy and desire through Terra's body. It was that she'd been avoiding. Part of that was the feelings she still harbored for Tania, even though that relationship was destined to fail as their destinies weren't intertwined in a way that allowed them to be together. The most uncomfortable part that made her squirm was the undeniable and uncontrollable pull she felt. She felt it the day they kissed, same as she did now.

M'ra bowed low to Terra, making her feel all sorts of uncomfortable. M'ra was the oldest and most powerful creature in any realm and she was showing subservience to Terra? Embarrassed, red filled her cheeks.

"You're the Minister. I'm nothing. What are you doing?"

M'ra lifted the veil over her face, turning her colorful eyes to Terra. Her pale skin matching the sandy rocks surrounding them. Her hair a deep red like the sky. Even though she'd died and lived a second life as a vampire she'd never lost the physical traits gained as a realm walker. Somewhere, that part of her still existed. "Save my realm."

What? The sky turned shades of pink until it glowed a golden yellow, pushing the red glow of Blood River away. Tears threatened Terra's eyes as she realized what was happening. It was too late. Sunshine spread over the realm and its heat burned through M'ra. Flames nipped at Terra.

"No!" she screamed. Pain and anger rising inside her like a boiling cauldron. Her mind churning with so much red and anguish she couldn't think. Turning her attention to the battlefield, ready to burn all who spread sunlight. She gulped at the destruction of lives and, from a place further out, circling the mess below stood warlocks, hands pressed outward. Radiation strong as the sun hurling over the field. Vampires puddled to the ground in agony. They weren't Lols vampires, but those of Drakonia, missing the mark that gave them the ability to walk in daylight. Terra's brain screamed.

In a mindless, anguished frenzy she squeezed Hank's hand and curled her open hand, creating a forcefield around them. Letting go of his hand she knelt at M'ra's side, fire curling against her skin as parts of her dropped into ash. "M'ra," she choked. "How do I save you?"

"Save… the… realm," M'ra choked out as flames licked her face until nothing was left but ashes. Terra sobbed, tears flowing into the heap of ashes that was, moments ago, M'ra, the oldest being alive. Her tears swirled into the dust, creating a milky puddle that trickled toward the edge of the plateau circling around an object. Terra reached down and plucked the object from the ground. A red stone set in a golden band. It was M'ra's. She slipped it on her finger and stood.

Facing Hank, tears streaming her face, anger bubbling in her soul. He put out his hands. She nodded and curled her fingers around his. Together they built up the forcefield they created. It grew around them as more and more energy pulled into it.

Clyde slid down her shoulder and curled on top of their joined hands as if he too could help. The sky turned dark as they gathered every ounce of energy and magic they could harness, sending the forcefield outward in an explosion. Ripples crested the atmosphere and over the ground. It swept all those who didn't belong and pushed them through the veil that widened as each vampire, warlock, and werewolf went through, then shrunk and vanished. The crimson sky returned as Terra and Hank collapsed.

28

Streams of red stretched across the creamy-colored ceiling as Terra opened her eyes. Beneath her, a soft mattress. A hunter green comforter up to her chin. She pushed upwards on her elbows and studied her surroundings. The dark-colored walls and décor turned her mind to the Minister's tower.

Clyde? Panic clutched her as she studied the room, finding shiny dress shoes a foot or so from the bed she lay in, up the gray slacks and green dress shirt, meeting Bane's gaze. "You're awake."

She had no use for conversation with him. She wanted Clyde, needed to know he was safe. In the bubble of energy she and Hank created, Clyde joined them. She shouldn't have taken him. A bowling ball of dread formed in her gut.

"Where's Clyde?"

"He's fine. No harm has come to him or will come to him."

Anything that came from Bane's mouth was little comfort to Terra. "Why isn't he here with me?"

The sound of Bane's voice was worse than nails on a chalkboard. "He will be. Right now he is… with the injured. He bites anyone who tries to take him away."

Terra chuckled. Clyde wasn't a biter, but if he thought he needed to be there then he wasn't going to let anyone take him away. Cold metal pressed against her finger, driving her thoughts back to M'ra and the explosion of energy she and Hank created. The vampires, there were so many on the sandy desert battlefield. *How many suffered werewolf bites? How many were scorched from the sun?* She couldn't lie in the bed when others needed help.

Pushing the covers off, the comforter dangling over the bed, she pulled her legs over the side.

"What do you think you're doing?" Bane asked in a tone that sounded concerned.

Not Bane. When had he ever been concerned for her or anything that didn't include bettering something for himself? "I'm leaving. My blood can save the vampires. You can stay here and do nothing," her words bit, "but I'm going to save some lives. As many as I can."

With a palm, he pushed her down. "No, you aren't. You are weak from expending so much energy. You must eat and rest to be any good for any of them."

He was right. She was weak. It wasn't his vampire strength that pushed her back onto the bed. It was her spent body that wasn't much more than a fragile glass doll. No, she had to do something. She couldn't let more die. M'ra, with her dying breath, asked her to save the realm. The cold metal of her ring pressed against the skin of Terra's finger. "Bring me food then take me to them."

"You are too important. If you give all you have then you will die and save no one. You must eat and rest. I promise you the vampires will survive at least until tomorrow then I will take you to them and you can save them all."

A reluctant sigh escaped her lips. She hated to admit the superficial vampire was right. "Fine."

Bane didn't leave her side as she ate. Normally she ordered but the meal in front of her was brought in. Filleted fish, steamed vegetables, and couscous, with a tall glass of fresh orange juice. She guessed they covered all the food groups in order to build up her strength. If she'd been left to order her own dinner it would have been layered in carbs.

It felt like Bane was babysitting her. She didn't need one. At seventeen, almost eighteen, she could take care of herself. Of course, that wasn't it. He was there to be sure she stayed there. The simple girl from San Francisco saved the entire realm and now she had a guard. How would M'ra feel about that? She'd be the one to post him there. What was she thinking? M'ra adored her and kept a close eye on her. That's why Bane was always lurking. "I can eat on my own."

He pressed his back into the chair as he dropped his leg. "I miss her too, but she knew what she was doing. It's not natural to live hundreds of years, even as a vampire. It was her time, she felt it."

Guilt twisted in her guts. She should have saved her. "What happens now?"

He glanced downward at his shoes then met her gaze. "There's really nothing you could have done. Vampires grow stronger with age and power. Immortality becomes a careful balance and they succumb to death easier than in their youth… The ring you're wearing will choose a new leader."

Terra had been under the impression the Minister position went to the eldest vampire. She pushed her thumb against the band. "What do you mean?"

He moved to the edge of the bed, the comforter bunching around him as he sat. "The ring sees into the hearts of vampires and makes a choice based on a vampire's strength of character." He paused, gazing into her eyes as if he could read her thoughts. "She was the oldest vampire because she was minister for so long. If Minister passed from eldest to eldest the vampire wouldn't necessarily have the strength for the job. Ruling a realm isn't easy. In the past, vampires fought for the position, killing one another over it. Their reigns short, until the ring was taken from our maker's dead boney finger. Since, it has chosen who reigns."

The crimson sky shining on the red stone sent a kaleidoscope of red shades across the room as she wiggled her finger, suddenly uncomfortable about wearing it.

"A ceremony will be staged and the ring will guide you to the next minister."

"Me?" she shot back. "I'm not a vampire."

"No, but you have the ring. Slide it off your finger."

Terra pulled at the ring. It wouldn't budge other than twist on her finger. She couldn't remove it.

"It's chosen you to help it find the next Minister. It won't come off your finger until that vampire is found. A red light will shine from the stone when that vampire touches you and the ring will easily slip off your finger, ready to be placed on the new minister's finger."

The bite of fish going down uneasy as she thought about the responsibility she bore to find the new minister and save the dying vampires. She pushed the bed tray away from her. "I guess I need my rest then."

She curled onto her side as Bane flipped the light. The door opened and closed, meaning he'd gone, but she didn't assume there wasn't a vampire posted outside the door. Most definitely there was. The protective creatures they were, one or more vampires would be watching her night and day.

29

Fur brushed against her face. She peered with one eye at the creamy face and chocolate trim of Clyde's ear. She rolled onto her chest, bringing him with her as she wrapped her arms around him. "I didn't forget you." She pulled him upwards, staring into his eyes. "How did you get here?"

The door closed and Bane stood by it. She laughed out loud to see him, in his freshly pressed posh suit and shined shoes, carrying a tray. Clyde took the opportunity to wriggle from her grasp and slip under the covers.

"We recovered him for you once he stopped trying to bite." Bane turned his eyes upwards as he spoke, like he was embarrassed to show emotion.

Terra pushed herself against the headboard, pulling a couple pillows behind her for padding. "Thank you."

A short smile flashed across his face. "After you eat and dress, I'll take you to the vampires in need of your blood."

"One more thing," she stated. He paused at the door and turned to face her. "What about Hank?"

"He helped you save the realm. He's being treated well and is asking to see you."

She swallowed, memories flooding her brain. "He's not coming, is he?"

He raised a trimmed eyebrow. "Not if you don't want him to."

It wasn't that she didn't want to see Hank. He was the peanut butter to her jelly, but the thing between them wasn't natural. In a short time she'd learned so much and being "fated" or whatever they were was too much.

After a breakfast of fruit, pancakes, and the creamiest scrambled eggs she'd ever eaten, she showered and pulled on a pair of jeans and a blouse left for her on the chair beside the bed. Clyde by her side, she went with Bane to the medi-vampire clinic set up on the battlefield itself. Some were in such bad shape they couldn't move them far.

Vampires lay in rows of beds. Some charred badly. Their flesh missing, bones protruding, faces bubbled from the burns, and limbs gone, ash, like M'ra. She blinked her eyes to stave away the tears. Her heart belonged to each and every one of them.

Intravenous blood was fed to them from bags to heal their wounds. The burn victims didn't need her blood. Human blood would heal their wounds.

Bane's voice cut through her thoughts: "It'll take time, but they'll recover, every limb will heal with a steady diet of blood and a concoction offered by the elves."

"And the ones bitten?"

He pulled back a curtain separating the areas. She pressed her hands against her mouth. Seeing charred vampires hanging onto their second life was horrible. Her stomach did somersaults seeing the ones bitten. Words couldn't describe it. Black ran through their veins, visible from where she stood. She swallowed hard. "You made me wait. Look at them! They've been suffering all night when I could have saved each one of them."

He gave her a look like her father did when she suggested something outrageous or overly dramatic. A sudden awkwardness as she'd just related Bane to her father, she glanced away from him.

"You still can." He walked her toward a chair and waved a hand for her to sit. "It isn't as bad as it looks. It turns out werewolves are at least part commoner so their bite isn't as toxic."

"What he says is true. They are in pain but it's not lethal yet," said a female vampire in scrubs, her long, dark hair pulled back in a ponytail and a warm smile on her face. "I was a nurse in my first life. They will live to finish their second life." Her voice had a calming effect on Terra as she leaned back in the chair, putting her arm out willingly to give her blood. Remembering all too clearly the young Lols vampire she saved from a lycan bite. It would take a lot of blood, but she was willing to give it.

"Terra!" screamed a familiar voice as Hyacinth rushed towards her. Her straight, dark hair pulled into a ponytail that swished side to side as she ran. The tent opening falling into place behind her.

"What is she doing here?" snarled a male vampire, his eyes deep pools of boiling tar. He rose from across the room to step in front of Terra. His eyes dropping to the ring on her finger.

In a second, Bane closed the distance between him and the other vampire. "She saved our realm, her blood can save each of the bitten and she carries the minister's ring. What she wants, what she needs, she gets," his words flaming with venom.

The other vampire flared his nostrils then stepped back. He didn't have to say any more as his words flung expletives her way. Bane was growing on her. All this time she'd despised him, been annoyed with him, and now he fended off angry vampires and gave her fatherly glances.

"Oh my gawd, oh my gawd." Hyacinth flung her arms around Terra, strands of straight, dark hair falling into Terra's face. "Are you OK?" She pulled back, her eyes fixed on Terra's.

"I'm fine," Terra grasped her friend's hand. "Really."

Hyacinth's gaze shifted downward. "So, it's true." She lifted Terra's hand. The red stone of the minister's ring catching the light in the tent.

"Yes." She couldn't, and didn't try to, hide the remorse she felt.

Over the course of the next two weeks they allowed Terra to donate a certain amount of blood daily and, day by day, the bitten vampires got better. There weren't many; seven in total. The charred vampires' flesh and bone grew back. At first, Terra had to hold in her gagging. It was a reflex, but it didn't stop her from being there. She ate a steady diet determined by the nutritionists in the kitchen. Three solid meals a day. They made sure she got plenty of rest. Hyacinth and Clyde stayed at Terra's side.

REALM WALKER

After a couple days, she was ready to face Hank. Seeing him wasn't the problem. It was M'ra's words that confirmed that what she and Hank had was supernatural. A destiny she couldn't escape. M'ra warned that something worse was ahead, something she and Hank had to battle together. If she'd learned anything, it was she couldn't avoid fate. It had a way of finding a path.

30

Dressed in ancestral regalia, Terra made her way down the steps of the minister's tower. She felt Hank's eyes on her as she made her way down the steps. A sense of pride to be something worshiped was shadowed by the idea of being worshiped. M'ra wasn't the most powerful being in all the realms, Terra was, and it made her skin crawl. It was far more responsibility than she wanted or needed, yet destiny wasn't escapable.

Taking the last step, she held her hand out and, as told, each vampire knelt and touched her hand as she went. The walk ahead of her long, as each of age vampire had to touch her hand. She took in a deep breath as the full breadth of their customs filled her up.

The single row of vampires was endless. The ring not finding a suitor for at least a mile, followed by another mile, and possibly a third, when the ring finally beamed into the crimson sky. She gazed at the vampire who didn't look any older than herself. His youthful face handsome, with a sharp chin and straight nose. He stayed in the kneeling position as she pulled the ring off her finger as instructed. His eyes fixed on the ground below.

She pushed the ring onto his finger and lifted his hand with hers. He stood, and together they held the ring high in the air. Each vampire she passed rose like falling dominoes in reverse and bowed to their new minister, along with the ones she hadn't passed.

A celebration continued for the remainder of the day and into the night, blood flowed like wine as vampires danced.

A glass of actual wine in her hand, she set it down as the new minister insisted on a dance. "Of course, Minister Jukane." With his brown skin and cerulean eyes, he was a beautiful creature. Vampires parted as she walked hand in hand with him.

He was a different ruler than M'ra. She was private, concealing her true identity for centuries. Jukane was far more transparent. A certain set of eyes burned into the back of her head.

Placing a hand on her back, he led. "This is probably strange to you."

Strange didn't begin to cover it, overwhelmed at being part of something bigger than herself, compassion in saving each bitten vampire who tonight celebrated with the rest of the realm. Her heart was filled so full it overflowed. "It's kind of a lot."

He whispered in her ear: "That's an understatement."

She chuckled. So many times in the past few months she'd thought just that.

"While you were saving vampires, I was getting to know someone who I think you know. Nice guy, crazy about you." He lifted her hand and spun her, coming face to face with Hank. "I leave you with my friend." The minister bowed and stepped away.

"You, he's talking about you. You and him…" She fumbled over her words.

Hank snaked an arm around her back. His braided hair pulled into a low ponytail showing off his strong jawline. A white silk dress shirt covering his chest and shoulders. Aftershave tickled her nose and brought back the desires she felt whenever they were close. "He's a nice guy. We talked. They accept you, but they don't accept me. It was warlocks with sun runes that caused so much damage. They snub their noses at me, same as you. I thought we had something. I know we do. We are connected. He didn't push me away but pulled me in. I think that's why the ring chose him."

Terra didn't know much about who or why the ring chose anyone, but Hank was right. She'd snubbed him along with the vampires, always running away, having somewhere else to be or something to do. It wasn't until last night she'd managed the courage to face him today. "You're right, I've been avoiding you. Not intentionally dissing you. I'm sorry."

He pulled her closer to him, until their bodies touched. "You have a habit of lying, and you're quite good at it, but I can see through it. We are meant to be and no matter how much you avoid me you can't hide from your heart."

Ugh! Why was he right?! She hadn't exactly been hiding… Yes, she had. Her mind had so much to consider. This all-powerful realm walker thing, and then being only half of the whole she-bang, she needed him. He was her other half. Two weeks of thinking about it, she still wasn't sure what it meant.

He leaned his head down, his soft lips brushing her ear. "You can't avoid whatever this is between us forever." A tingling sensation worked its way from her ear to her feet as his lips left her lobe. His dark eyes searched hers and the music and celebration drifted away as all her attention focused on him. He lowered his head, his lips pressed against hers with a thirst, a hunger, that matched her own.

The rhythm of her pulse pumped in her head. The energy of the second heartbeat thumped in every muscle and fiber of her body. Her mind swelled with emotion and desires she hadn't thought were possible. A connection she couldn't deny. The realms spun on an axis and fireworks exploded through her being as the world suddenly froze and it was only the two of them.

31

The Tribunal

flags for each realm hung at their points from the circular walls of Provence Hall. The vampires had asked her to stay. She couldn't hide in Drakonia indefinitely. If being a realm walker was a crime, they would have to punish her.

Rosette's thin lips pinched together like a clamp. Her face contorted with concern, eyes filled with compassion. She wasn't worried about being banished to Lols. She was worried about Terra and what the tribunal might decide. They could banish her, or cleanse her as they had the others.

Hidden Passages

Terra and Hank saved Drakonia but she feared it wouldn't be enough. Their display of sheer power was the talk of every realm and the words 'realm walker' were whispered and spread in solemn, hushed tones. People were scared, yet grateful for what she and the warlock had done. For the past eighteen years the words 'realm walker' had been forbidden. Their contributions erased from history. The young lived a life without knowledge of the realm walkers.

Terra was a new generation of realm walker and, with her connection to the warlock, was stronger than anything the realms had seen. Rosette didn't understand the connection between them but she hadn't forgotten all the good realm walkers had done, nor Terra's mother – realm walker of Aradia and keeper of the Serenity Tree. Nor had she forgotten Cyrus, Terra's biological father. A man whose narcissism was solely responsible for the cleansing of realm walkers. He'd gone so far as to assist Terra's parents' escape then demand Terra's mother take him to his child.

It wasn't fatherly love but a darkness that filled his heart when he realized the death of each realm walker didn't feed and satiate his power. The only explanation was that the power culminated in his child. Rosette never saw Terra's mother again, nor did anyone ever find Cyrus. His name wasn't spoken, as if ignoring that he may be alive kept everyone safe.

Hank stood by Terra's side. His shoulders squared as he stood tall and proud. Together, they'd been through more than Rosette imagined the day she'd sent Terra to M'ra. Water built up behind her eyes as she fought the tears of pride she felt for Terra and Hank.

The young man risked everything to save a realm not his own, to desert his own people. His entire life toppled. No longer did he have a home as he couldn't return to Lols and the warlocks. Surely, he'd face a horrible punishment for betraying them. The vampires weren't friendly to him, even though they offered for him to stay. It was only because he did help save them, even if the rest of his kind tried to destroy them.

Terra showed no fear beside the tall warlock. It wasn't her first time before the tribunal. The teen made uncomfortable waves since the moment she arrived. She'd take whatever they dished out. Holding her head high, with her shoulders back, she said, "I stand here before you as something you hate, something you destroyed, yet somehow I was hidden amongst commoners, raised by a loving father. I am why the realms stand, why they weren't toppled in your haste to destroy those you feared."

The gravity of what she said next settled on her shoulders and silence persisted. "I am the last realm walker and he is my guardian."

A proud smile came over Rosette as she fought the tears in her eyes. Everything Terra said was true. Should they have cleansed every realm walker, the realms would have toppled. It was Merla's warning when she created them with the level 4 spell. In her gut, Rosette understood, as every diplomat and adult who lived through the cleansing did, that the veils didn't weaken until after the cleansing.

Lukas, the eldest lycan, stood, followed by the other four Canidan diplomats. He stepped forward into the center circle, hands behind his back. "It isn't a crime to be born. If it wasn't for this realm walker and warlock the realms wouldn't be at peace. We were invaded." His tone rose as he turned and faced the diplomats. "Because of them, we can return to our lives. They sent every commoner vampire, werewolf, and warlock to Lols and sealed the veil between our realms. I speak for every lycan when I say I have extreme gratitude for these two who stand before us. Let this be a vote. Stand with me if you agree we owe them our lives."

The room returned to silence, followed by the rising of each diplomat from every realm.

"It is settled, you are free to go," Lukas said. He turned to Terra and Hank. Taking Terra's hand he cupped his large hands over it. "You are a brave young woman and are always welcome in Canida." Letting go of her hand he placed a large hand on Hank's shoulder. "You also have a home in Canida but I don't think you'll be needing one, as this young woman will keep you busy." He smiled at them both and stepped away.

Latisha – Northeastern Regional Warlock Wizard

Problems had ways of solving themselves. The battle was fruitless. The mission to uncover the stones and watch the fae squirm failed miserably. What came of it was something else. A new sense of entitlement. Her warlocks, along with the wolves and vampires, had been forced by an explosion back to the human realm. A phenomenon that became known as the expelling.

A teenager and Latisha's "lost" warlock reportedly teamed up. Their power so great an explosion erupted from them and blasted everyone through the veil into their birth realm. It wasn't a lost cause. Her suspicions were correct. Hank had the source rune and with it a power beyond all other warlocks. He could present himself to the source without suffering a painful death.

Her mind recalled the rash of disappearances approximately twenty years previous. Wolves, vampires, and warlocks vanished; she'd come to blame those in the realms slipping through the veils. It was the tragedy that drove the factions together. Most days they didn't like one another, but they had a common unknown enemy. There was always strength in numbers. The vanishings stopped abruptly and together, in the present day, they fought the enemy.

Latisha rolled her shoulders forward in a shrug and lifted her feet to the table. It wasn't something she did in front of others. She didn't need Hank or the Stones of Hovrath. In the human realm things were shaping up nicely. Magic was no longer a secret as rumors spread like wildfire through the night world and now day world communities.

The warlocks, wolves, and vampires were finally on the same side. Influencers used #awakening all over social media, with videos and memes. Those with magic were gathering, building in number. Her sights were set on sucking in these hybrids, giving them a strong shoulder and bountiful training. They were hers for the molding. None would ever be warlocks, but they had their own talents and the human realm was hers for the taking.

Hidden Passages

In time, Hank would learn the power of the source rune and everything she built here would have a purpose. The warlocks would finally have a way home.

To be continued…

Ring of Betrayal
REALM WALKER VOL. 4

1

Northeastern Regional Wizard

Terra trapped the plasma beam extending from Hank's hands and amplified it, transmitting it into the sky. It spiraled through the clouds until it reached the veil. Lavender light cascaded down the edges of the veil, the rest bounced back. She caught it in one hand and pushed it back to him. It fizzled and vanished as his body absorbed it.

She ripped the seams of the realm open and slipped into the inbetween, emerging behind him. He spun as the realm opened and caught her hands in his. Blue energy grew around him. Terra absorbed it, feeling the warm plasma encapsulate them. Together they forced it outward, the blast pushing the trees backwards. The sound of branches snapping echoed across the highlands.

She could play with magic all day. Her command grew with each practice. They'd taken to training in remote areas. The highest peak of Sier within the toppled palace was one of her favorites. The crisp, freezing air whistled in her ears and excited the warm energy between them.

Hank spun Terra around, his braids whipping through the air. She leaned back to avoid being hit with them. He pushed a plasma blade against her throat as she leaned. She smiled and pushed her hands around the flat sides, forcing it away from her as she squared her shoulders. She folded it into a ring and forced it into the snow.

A blue glow snaked around their legs, pulling them together. He let out a scream so high-pitched her ears barely registered it. She gathered the sound waves and forced them into the ground. The earth shook beneath their feet and the force of the rumble cracked the base of the fallen castle, running along the side until what was left of the one remaining upright tower crumbled to the ground.

She enveloped them in a protective shield as he lost his balance and fell onto her. His hands pressed against the bottom of the shield as their eyes locked.

His firm, muscled legs rested against hers and his face was elevated a few inches above her forehead. His warm breath melted against her and she felt the gentle movement of his chest rise and fall as he breathed. The attraction between them growing since the moment their lips met months ago.

Terra lifted her chest and sat up on her elbows. Inches between their mouths. In the clear blue, cloudless sky a dragon soared over them. Its wingspan alone was magnificent. Its outline soft and fuzzy from the fog working its way around the inside of the shield. "I think that's enough for today." She dropped the shield and felt her body fall against the firm, icy earth.

His eyes moved from hers to her chest before he pushed off the ground and offered her a hand.

She wanted to grab his shirt, not his hand, and pull him closer, but fought the urge. He was her guardian, but he was more. Her power was mighty, but with his strength hers was doubled. M'ra's words about a greater danger before dropping into a pile of ash festered in Terra's head. Whatever was happening between her and Hank was important, yet she hadn't completely given in to him. As much as she wanted to, a part of her warned against it.

This nagging festered inside her. There was always a catch. Things weren't as they seemed. She hadn't returned to Lols since she sealed the veils and spent most days after classes training with Hank. They still needed the exit Stones of Hovrath and would have to return to Lols to find them. The enter stones were stolen from under their noses by the lottery winning, millionaire, baker, fae/warlock hybrid, Terina.

They managed to get them back and Terra kept them hidden in a world she'd molded in the inbetween. A place only she could get to, unless she brought invited guests.

She dropped the protective shield around Clyde. It's how she kept him safe when they practiced. Clyde scampered between them and stretched his long body along her leg. She reached down to grab him and he scampered away, poking his head into her backpack. A big hint he was ready to go home.

"They might notice this," Hank said, arms folded across his chest as he eyed the fallen tower.

She twisted her mouth. She could fix this. With her hands, she commanded the rubble to slide back into place. Piece by piece lifted from the ground and climbed. What was left of the framing dropped into its slot.

Hank placed his hands on her shoulders to feed her more energy. His touch sent a wave of yearning and distracted her for a moment. A rock slid down before she caught it and sent it climbing again. This was getting ridiculous. She wanted him, but it wasn't right. Not yet. The stones climbed and dropped faster. They didn't stop until the entire palace was restored. Magic was foreplay and eased the desires burning inside her.

They returned to Provence Academy before the fake sun lowered, in time for dinner. It was great to see all her friends, both purebloods and hybrids, laughing as they sat around the two tables they pulled together. In Lols she'd collected five hybrids for the tribunal. That was her mission. They were to become new members, bringing the diplomat total to forty.

For the past few months they'd been learning about the history of the tribunal and the breadth of their jobs. They'd also been learning to command magic, something they'd started on their own in Lols, but at Provence Academy, with trained instructors, they'd reached new peaks.

Mario had learned much control over his shifting. Meesha's guidance had probably been more responsible than what he learned at the academy. Meesha was a pureblood lycan. Strong, powerful, trustworthy, and a great friend.

Alex had come a long way. He had more command over his visions but he insisted some things he wasn't meant to see until the time was right. He'd also warned Terra when they met that powerful people were after her. She couldn't help the chills that spiked her arms when she put his words and M'ra's together.

Warlita, who'd already mastered enchanting magical objects such as stones and precious metals, also had a unique ability to remold metal and rocks as if they were pottery clay.

Dena's ability to speak with insects extended beyond insects. She could communicate with some animals too and was learning to control the power of suggestion. It was a skill she was developing, but mostly it happened when she least expected. Terra thought it worked much like the vampires' ability to mind bend.

Kenya was quickly becoming a master of curses, sigils, and making things move with her mind.

Some of their magic wasn't allowed in Provence but, as hybrids, they had easy access to the realms they were a part of which Terra took upon herself to help them find out.

It was a field trip when the five were first allowed to stay. They went from realm to realm. Terra figured it would help them define and fine tune their command of magic. The bonus was that they often went to the other realms to practice level 3 magic. What surprised Terra the most was how they were able to enter each realm like Hank, which she didn't have an explanation for either. In the end, it didn't matter. What mattered was connecting with their magic so they one day could be good Lols diplomats because they understood their strengths and weaknesses.

2

Dr. Carina leaned against her desk, one long leg over the other. Her dark hair braided and piled on top of her head, a few loose curls fell across the sides of her face. "The Great War was a time of distrust and pain among the realms. As healers, the elves worked overtime creating new serums and salves to heal those in every realm. It was a time of great discovery, as well as overwhelming sadness."

Terra's mind ventured in another direction as she already knew of the Great War and why her kind were created. The lecture wasn't about realm walkers, it was about Elfin history. The great healers.

A tug on her arm brought her mind to Clyde, who was wearing his harness. It helped keep him out of trouble in the class. The leash looped around her wrist. She glanced down but didn't see him. *Clyde,* she called in her mind. Another pull on her arm almost sent her falling out of her chair. She braced her hands on the table and spotted Clyde. His head and front paws were buried in another student's backpack.

She pulled her arm, catching his attention. He glanced at her with his bandit eyes and chocolate ears then leapt out of the backpack, something in his mouth. She gave him the look and he curled beneath her seat.

It wasn't the first time he was curious in class, after all he was a ferret, it was in his nature. Occasionally he took Halsey's sparkly hair pieces and hid them under her bed. The spiteful glare on Halsey's flawless face was worth not scolding him for it. She leaned her arm down for whatever was in his mouth. He dropped it on the floor and it clinked like a ring dropping onto tile, and he chittered lightly at her. She sat up as Dr. Carina glanced her way.

Terra pulled her feet in front of Clyde so no one would see whatever he dropped on the floor. It barely made a sound. Elves didn't have as exceptional hearing as wolves, dragons, and lycans so she doubted anyone but her heard it.

When class ended, she gathered her books and notepad. Dr. Carina's heels clicked on the floor as she drew closer to Terra. "I like Clyde as much as the next person, but if he can't behave himself he needs to stay in your dorm during class," she said with a warning tone.

"I'm sorry. His fur tickled my leg is all. It won't happen again," Terra explained, curious as to what he'd found and dropped on the floor.

Dr. Carina nodded then turned on her heel and strolled to her desk. Terra used that moment to collect what Clyde had taken. Between his paws was something that looked like a feather pen, but the feather was made of metal. He nipped at her as she tried to take it.

She held in a squeak and shook her hand. The surface of her skin wasn't broken, but there was a small pink spot from his teeth. He'd never nipped at her before. She collected her backpack and let him carry whatever treasure it was he'd found.

As she stepped into the hall, Deena, who was also in the class was waiting for her. "What was that about?"

"The pitfalls of having a ferret."

Deena's eyes dropped to Clyde. "What's that thing he's carrying?"

"His new treasure."

The courtyard and cafeteria were full. She handed Meesha the handle to Clyde's harness and warned, "Don't try and take the thing in his mouth." She always had to leave him outside the cafeteria since the dragon lady cafeteria manager scuffle.

Alex and Warlita were at the kiosk. Since their arrival the school had expanded the kiosk, and added a toaster oven - which meant crispy fries - and a larger refrigerator and freezer. She grabbed a turkey sandwich and a raspberry yogurt.

A smile played on her lips as she watched Halsey, her fae diama or princess of Navarin roommate, and Bjorn. Terra held herself responsible for the match up. It was the book she found in Navarin that led them on a scavenger hunt to find the realm grimoire, and a bit more. They'd been stuck like superglue since.

Halsey puckered her lips in a pouty face as he stole some kind of food from her plate. As far as Terra could tell it was a playful love/hate relationship and would probably end when the school year was over. Halsey would return to Navarin and learn to be a ruler, as one day she'd be Queen, and Bjorn? Who knew. He'd probably return to Navarin as well. His mom was a scientist, but she didn't think that put him high enough on the peerage scale for them to continue dating, at least not publicly.

"Mlaka flae," Kenya said as she strolled to the table and took her seat. Since Terra's friend group grew by five, the entire group grew by five.

Kayln giggled. "Be careful what you say out loud in old fae."

Deena glanced at the two, with an eyebrow raised as if to ask *What did she say?*

Kayln blew it off as she lifted a sandwich-type fae food to her mouth. "What's that thing in Clyde's mouth?"

Terra expelled a frustrated gust of air before explaining. "I don't know. He pulled it out of someone's backpack and won't let me touch it."

"That's not like Clyde," Caspen offered as he sat down, placing his tray with some type of elfin wrap on it on the table. His large, curly afro bouncing as he sat.

Terra shrugged. She had no answer. He was a ferret. It was weird, but she was sure he'd drop it when he got bored with it.

After lunch, Alex grabbed Terra's arm before she stood. "You need to get that away from Clyde. It's enchanted." He had unique abilities and one of them was the ability to see words, even though he was blind, as well as future events with a bit of DNA.

This put Terra on alert. "What is it saying? Is he under a spell of some kind?"

Always quiet and mostly solemn, his face tightened more than usual. "I don't understand the language."

There was only one place Terra could think of and only one person in Provence she knew to ask. Professor Gwond, her quirky troll magic instructor. He was a walking encyclopedia, brimming over with knowledge of magic. Since the expelling he'd been teaching her level 3 magic. They'd meet in

Verboten. She'd learned to transform, as he called it, into other creatures which she'd had some practice with during the invasion. She hadn't brought up the Stones of Hovrath. No real reason, or maybe there was. After the invasion, losing M'ra, M'ra's warning, and the undefined thing between her and Hank, she'd been more reserved.

She returned to her room after lunch and caught up on her homework while she waited for Gwond's office hours. Waiting for Clyde to put down the feather pen, but every time she glanced his way he picked it up and went somewhere else in the room. His behavior was distressing.

She felt like a worried mother by the time she entered Gwond's office. He lifted his head slightly, his round eyes peered at her from behind his glasses. He seemed to read the distress in her expression. "Ms. O'Malley. Is there a problem?"

She blurted it out, as her concern for Clyde was overwhelming. "It's Clyde." Gwond raised his torso and glanced over his desk. "That pen thing in his mouth. He found it in class and won't let go of it. Alex says it's talking to him. When I tried to get it from him, he nipped at me."

With a finger over his mouth, Gwond stood and walked around his desk. The plumage on his tail reached over and stroked Clyde and he chanted something. Clyde growled with the pen in his mouth. A full-on growl. She'd never heard him do that. He was a ferret, not a dog.

"I see." He looked at the clock. "Follow me." His blue sneakers squeaked with each step on the shiny floor.

They walked down the hall and to the first floor, reaching the room under the stairs. The septagonal room with a flag representing each of the seven realms. He peered right, then left. "You are a realm walker." His plumage pointed toward the ceiling. "As a realm walker, there are things you should know and only you can do what I'm going to ask you to do."

She narrowed her eyes. Gwond didn't always follow the rules. It was what she liked best about him.

"Press your hand under each flag."

She did and, after doing so, the floor beneath them dropped, catching her stomach. "What is this? What was that?"

He stepped off the platform. "The antiquity room."

Light from sconces illuminated various objects on the walls and on tables. The floor-elevator rose back into place so quietly someone could only hear it if they were close by. "What are all these?" she asked in awe.

He pointed towards swords hanging from the wall in leather sheaths. "These were used in the Great War. Some are covered in wolf blood. They were used to kill vampires. Those arrows," he pointed at a few quivers on a table, "soaked in vampire blood."

"What about this?" Terra pointed at an object that looked oddly familiar. It was shaped like a gear for a pocket watch, only it was missing something, oval, and about the size of a rock.

"Part of an ascendant, probably used to travel to Lols." He paused for a moment then continued. "Most of history has been lost and lives in what is left of these artifacts. As a realm walker, you need to understand what life was like before realm walkers, but first we need to free your ferret."

Ascendant – that wasn't a new word. She had seen something about one… Her mind cycled, but was more focused on her ferret. Gwond picked up a small, square, wooden box with a key in the lock from one of the tables and placed it on the ground. Clyde scooted backwards, the feather pen tight in his mouth. His tiny eyes fixed on the box as Gwond pulled out the key and pushed the lid back then walked a couple steps backwards.

Clyde moved closer to the box and paused, glancing at Gwond before he scurried forward and peeked his head inside it. His mischievous ferret instincts couldn't ignore trouble and curiosity, which generally went together. Gwond chanted something and the lid dropped closed. It startled Clyde and his jaw slacked and the object fell inside. He barely managed to get his tiny, furry head out in time for the top to come all the way down. Gwond stuck the key back in the lock and twisted, then placed the box back where it came from.

Reading Terra's expression he explained: "The box attracts magic and traps it." She nodded.

Pressing a finger to his cheek: "Where was I?" His eyes twice their normal size through the thick glasses rolled upwards. "Yes, yes. Before realm walkers, all the artifacts had a place and a purpose. People didn't have the same connection to magic as we do now. In order to use it, these tools came in handy. Realm walkers amplify magic. They weren't only created to form and seal the veils."

He went on, explaining how realm walkers were created to be diplomats and they were good at it. If lycans needed Aradian wood to build something, the Canidan realm walker would make a deal with the Aradian realm walker. For generations, most realm walkers didn't understand their strength. That matched M'ra's words and it was the great, powerful and, in her opinion, unbalanced Cyrus that helped them realize their potential. Gwond continued explaining how they didn't understand that they were part of the source and amplified it. They fell in line and did as they were told.

It was news to Terra. There'd been clues, but none she caught on to. Possibly, it was down to the wild adventure and lack of sleep that many things were fuzzy. Maybe she'd heard them before, but couldn't readily recall.

Lols was alive with magic and M'ra warned her that she was part of the source. There was also the entire spell that formed realm walkers. It all pointed at realm walkers having a unique and strong connection to magic because they were the amplifications of the source. To her, it was overwhelming to think about.

Their existence had been erased and the artifacts stored below the school after the cleansing. They weren't allowed to ever speak of it. He painted a picture of Cyrus, the great realm walker who understood their connection to magic. How they were more than good little diplomats whose existence kept the veils strong. He understood they could manipulate the veils as they pleased, resize the realms if they pleased. There was no limit to what they could do. This scared the purebloods, as they weren't as powerful and dominant as they wished. Their weaknesses and flaws sticking out like a bruised thumb.

Realm walkers, as Gwond painted them, were superior in every way.

"People fear those they can't control," Gwond continued his monologue. He wanted a home for realm walkers, a place they could call theirs. He claimed they were slaves to the realms and should have free will to come and go as they pleased, not when they were ordered. Leaders of all the realms needed them. There was a small group of agitators that whispered in the ears of the leaders, played on their fears that somehow the realm walkers would take over and kill them to keep their realms for themselves. Momentum grew as leaders turned their backs on the realm walkers. They were imprisoned, but bars couldn't hold them, so they murdered them all and called it the cleansing.

After, they took every book that mentioned realm walkers, and all enchanted objects, and destroyed them, except the few that had been salvaged by realm walkers before the cleansing and stored in the antiquity room.

It seemed they salvaged a lot as she studied the books, scrolls, and objects. "I thought the school didn't exist until after the realm walkers were…" She couldn't say the word. Her mother was one of them.

He smiled. "You've been paying attention. Correct. The school didn't exist."

"Then how? I don't understand."

Realm Walker

A thoughtful expression formed on his face. He seemed eager to tell her more. "I will explain that one day. Now is not the time. All you need to understand is that history is important to preserve. You are the only person who can come down here. You may share it with the warlock. Some of these artifacts might be from his ancestors, but you mustn't show or tell anyone else."

She really hated how everyone referred to Hank as 'the warlock'. It was the equivalent of calling her 'the realm walker' instead of Terra. He had a name. She narrowed her eyes and corrected Gwond. "Hank."

As she spoke, her eyes studied the objects in the room. One in particular caught her eye. It was a pickaxe with a pearl handle. The axe head made of wood. "What's that for?" she asked, pointing to the pickaxe.

"Something dangerous. It's a reverser and pulls a soul from its harvested sphere," Gwond responded. His words lacked the caution she expected.

www.ingramcontent.com/pod-product-compliance
Lightning Source LLC
Chambersburg PA
CBHW060919190726
48286CB00002B/562